Praise for Soul-iloquy

"A soul-inspiring read! As a woman who has been honoring the whispers of her soul of her soul for over twenty-five years myself, I was drawn to Lily's character, reflective personality, and her journey of self-discovery. Kris Groth's book, *Soul-iloquy* will inspire you to trust, honor and follow your own soul whispers."

Linda Joy ~ Visibility Catalyst and Bestselling Publisher, Aspire Magazine and Inspired Living Publishing

"A gift from above! *Soul-iloquy* weaves powerful spiritual lessons into a beautiful story we can all relate to, as it takes you on a journey of soul-searching, self-discovery, and transformation. The angels have smiled upon Kris Groth with this book! **For all spiritual seekers, this book is a must read!"**

Sunny Dawn Johnston ~ Author, Speaker and Psychic Medium

"A wonderful story of love, honoring feelings, and the search to find an answer for life's questions. Lily's journey to understand her heart leads to a deep connection to her soul's wisdom and the knowledge she has support on many levels."

Rev Maggie Chula ~ Spiritual Minister and Healer for the Soul

"This beautiful work of art blends storytelling with profound wisdom and practical tools for living a deeply nurtured and authentic life. The way the story is written allows us to fully experience Lily's transformational journey through her journal entries, self-nurturing practices, and reflections on her growth and change. **It's a delightful and inspiring read!**"

Kelley Grimes, MSW ~ Counselor, Speaker and Bestselling Author

"With flowing prose, Kris invites us to share in Lily's journey of awakening. As a healer and teacher, I especially value Lily's journal entries (used to introduce each chapter) as examples of a person beginning to dialog with their own higher soul and guides. Lily's connection with Angels also creates a template for others longing to experience their own direct connection with these beneficent beings. **Brava, Kris, for creating a magical blend of romance, healing, spirituality and self-help!**"

Reba Linker ~ Healer, Author, Teacher

"In *Soul-iloquy,* we are taken on **a journey of self-discovery and soul-discovery.** Through Lily St. Angelo, Kris paints a vivid picture - the shining star is our deep personal reunion/relationship with our soul, connecting us to our most sacred path - True Love."

Debra Oakland ~ Courage Advocate & Bestselling Author of *Change Your Movie, Change Your Life: 7 Reel Concepts for Courageous Change*

"As I was reading Kris's penning, I was the woman in this book, *SOUL-ILOQUY*. What I share is this: It's essential for you to reconnect to that place inside of you where your intuition and where your truth is a the vital part of your life. **This is your SOUL."**

Cindy Hively ~ Intuitive Healing Coach

"I loved this book! It's such a beautiful expression of a woman's journey to the depths of her soul and how she can find the courage to express herself and follow her soul's path. Each of us have a yearning to connect and have a conversation with our soul. Kris Groth gives us this opportunity in her book, *Soul-iloquy*. Through her beloved character Lily, Kris takes us on a healing journey to connect with our soul. She asks the transformative questions that inspire an inner dialogue with our own soul as she guides us gracefully step-by-step, on our personal path to spiritual awakening. A must read for anyone seeking spiritual guidance in getting in touch with the deepest reaches of their soul."

Dr. Debra L. Reble ~ Intuitive Psychologist and International Bestselling Author

"A beautiful story of spiritual discovery. It's a loving invitation to dive deeper into healing, communication with your Soul, and Soul connections throughout time."

Shellie Nelson

"**Captivating!** This is Lily's story but, in reality, it is every woman's story who has been at the depths of heartache & pain. Her journey, our journeys, are never without challenges and we each have the opportunity to lead our lives through a deep connection to our inner truth and spirit. Kris Groth is able to draw the reader in and show us this connection through Lily's story and how we can all learn from Lily's experience to open our hearts, trust ourselves and have faith."

Laura Clark ~ Master Soul Coaching® Practitioner & Trainer. Founder of Soul Wise Living

"In Soul-iloquy, Kris Groth shares the story of Lily St. Angelo and while reading her story, I couldn't help but think that in many ways, it is all of our stories. All of us who've been on our own spiritual journey, will resonate with the questions that plague Lily, with her experiences finding the answers and with her surrender to connecting to a deeper part of herself—her soul. The book is both **charming and heartwarming**, filled with real-life situations familiar to us all. By navigating them with an open heart, mind and spirit, Lily reminds us **how rich life can be when we are finally living a soul-filled life!**"

Beverley Golden ~ Writer, Peacenik and Bestselling Author

Soul-iloquy

A Novel of Healing, Soul Connection & Passion

KRIS GROTH

Spiritual Mentor ~ Energy Healer ~ Bestselling Author

SOUL-ILOQUY

A Novel of Healing, Soul Connection & Passion

By Kris Groth

Copyright © 2018 Kris Groth

All rights reserved.

Transcendent Publishing
PO Box 66202
St. Pete Beach, FL 33736
www.transcendentpublishing.com

Transcendent
——Publishing——

ISBN-13: 978-1-7320764-0-2

Library of Congress Control Number: 2018942104

Printed in the United States of America.

Dedication

To all those seeking soul connection, passion and purpose ... may you have all the help and guidance you need, recognize and understand all messages you receive, and allow beauty to flow through your life in miraculous ways!

Contents

Letter To My Readers

Dear Reader,

I never really planned to write a book. I was meditating one night on the summer solstice, asking for guidance as to what was next for me. I received one of my clearest messages ever, that by this time next year, I would be writing a book. I thought, "Well, that's interesting. I'm not a writer and have no idea what I would write." So, I set it aside. Six months later ideas started flowing in about writing a novel; I jotted them down in a journal, and the journey began. A couple days before the next summer solstice, my rough draft of this book was completed. It has been divinely guided the whole way, with ideas, inspiration and helpful people showing up just when I needed them. I am so grateful and amazed!

I have been a student of spirituality, meditation, and soul connection practices for many years. I am so excited to share my wisdom and presence to help others on their soul's path, to find peace, purpose, and passion in life. It is my hope that by reading this story, you will receive the wisdom, lessons, and healing on deeper levels by being drawn in to the lives of the characters, and that loving energy will flow to you as you read. Each time you read it you may experience it differently, depending on your needs at the time.

My day job is working as an energy healer and spiritual mentor, so some of the characters and experiences in this book have been inspired by what I have seen in my work, through my clients' healing as well as my own. It is a work of fiction, though I hope you will be able to identify or recognize parts of yourself in these characters as they move through their journeys. I hope it will inspire you to continue with your own healing and soul connection.

I'm excited to have you with me on this miraculous journey!

Much love, light and gratitude to you,

Kris

Chapter 1

so·lil·o·quy sə 'liləkwē

Soliloquy: A noun, from the Latin roots, solus "alone" plus loqui "speak" meaning "talking to oneself."

Soul-iloquy: A noun, an adaptation of the word soliloquy, meaning "talking to one's soul."

~Lily's journal

L ily St. Angelo sat alone in her cozy one-bedroom apartment, the upstairs of a century-old house in Uptown Minneapolis. Wrapped up in a blanket in the middle of the day, not for warmth but for comfort and a sense of security, she lay down on her comfy couch. Hot tears roll down her face into her ears as she lays there. *"Please help me! I don't know what to do. I feel so empty, so lost. I have so much to be grateful for, I should be happy because I do have a great life, but I'm not. I don't even know what is missing or what I want. Please help me to find what it is that would make me happy, that would make my life seem worthwhile. I need*

help. I need guidance. Please help me to know what to do!" The words of her prayer flowed out of her as softly as her tears. When she'd finished, her body shook with her sobs. She felt as if she were breaking wide open from the inside. *"What is happening to me?"* Continuing to weep, she felt her sorrow and pent-up emotions leaving her, like wild birds being let out of a cage.

When she was a little girl, lounging on the hammock in her backyard, Lily dreamed of one day having a handsome husband who treated her like a queen, a job helping people in some way, a big beautiful house overlooking a lake, and a couple kids (a boy and a girl, of course). Now it seemed like this dream was close to becoming reality. *"Everything I've ever wanted is within my grasp, but I feel more lost than ever. What is wrong with me?"*

A golden light filled the room from no apparent source. All at once, she stopped crying. The emotional upheaval was gone, and a sense of calm and peace settled over her. Within this peace, a gentle lightness began to fill her. It came from above, a soft warmth and glow completely enveloping her, and the love she felt was almost overwhelming, a feeling so pure that her eyes started to tear, powerful and yet tender and comforting. A voice in her head, but not her own, said, *"You are not alone. We are always with you. You are being helped. Be open to the help that comes your way."* Filled with a serenity she had never experienced before, she lay with her eyes closed and let it all soak in. Hers lips curved in a peaceful smile; her spirit relaxed, as her exhaustion left. Her life would never be the same.

She had always believed in God and angels, but as empty words other people talked about. She grew up going to church because that's what everyone did, and she had no choice in the matter. It was never something that rang true for her, though. As an adult, she simply focused on living a good life, being kind to others, and being the best person she could be. Certainly, no religion could do better than that.

She slept for an hour or so, then woke up and decided to check her Facebook feed. The usual meaningless posts, a few inspirational quotes, skipping all political posts, a couple cute animal videos, then one stopped her cold.

"Are you feeling stuck in your life and 'just can't live this way' but aren't sure how to free yourself to move forward? Are you feeling lost and disconnected, not sure what steps to take to continue on your spiritual journey and find your purpose? Are you going through some big changes or transitions in your life and need help discovering what your soul really wants for you? Are you committed to doing whatever it takes to feel peace within yourself and find what makes your soul sing?"

It was an ad for a healer in the area who helps people to connect with their soul. Lily just couldn't turn away from this ad. This energy healer specialized in healing, soul connections, and spiritual transformation. She was only a couple miles away, too. The questions in the ad perfectly echoed what she was feeling, which kind of creeped her out, as if it was written just for her. She answered a big YES! to each one. The message came back to her about being open to the help that was coming her way. She clicked on the link and scheduled an appointment for the next day. As soon as it was confirmed, she released a big sigh of relief. Help is on the way!

The healer, Serena Rivers, was a woman in her mid-40's,

with mid-length hair of varying shades of brown with bits of gray mixed in like sparkles. She had a kind and radiant smile that immediately put Lily at ease. She had an indistinct look, but one thing that stood out about her was her eyes. Intense light gray eyes that could see into the depths of a person. Surprisingly, this was not uncomfortable, like one would expect, but it was as if she saw everything with loving acceptance. No need for pretending or hiding, it was all out there, reaffirming to Lily, she was in the right place.

Bathed in the warm glow of salt lamps, the room radiated a nurturing peace that wrapped her up like a cocoon. Quartz crystals hung from the ceiling as stars twinkling from above, along with rocks and crystals in a myriad of colors and forms, gave the room a powerful yet supportive vibe. Soft music of chimes and nature sounds floated through the air. Even the white cloud-like blanket on the massage table held a heavenly feel and supported the work that was to happen there. One couldn't help but feel relaxed, comforted and held upon walking into this healing room.

The session consisted of mainly energy healing, with Serena's hands gently resting on Lily's body. As soon as Serena's hands made contact, Lily sensed an electric current flowing through her body, a gentle warmth and tingling from her feet up through her head. Her body began to melt into the massage table where she lay, barely able to even sense her arms and legs. Then Serena began to speak softly, guiding her to connect with her center, with her core, grounding her to the earth ... feeling the energy flowing even more strongly from the earth up through her body, strengthening the previous current. She then opened up the flow through the top of Lily's head to connect with the divine and bring in even more healing energy. Now with this coming in through the top of her head, adding to and intensifying the energy in her body, Lily was radiating, buzzing, and felt like she was floating. It was an amazing feeling, hard to describe even as she was experiencing it.

Serena brought Lily's awareness to the light at the center of her core. A bright white light, brightest at the center, expanded and radiated out through the rest of her body, and also beyond her body to her energy field. "This light is the light of your soul, your spirit, your true essence, whatever term you prefer. It is always there. You can access it at any time." Lily saw the image of this light in her mind's eye, and could also feel the warmth and peace in that center. "Let yourself feel connected to your soul. Notice any sensations, emotions, any messages that come into your awareness."

"It feels like home. Like this is where I belong. How can that be when this isn't a place?"

"It is your true home. It is where your true self lives. I have a feeling there's a part of you that has been longing to find this. You are being reunited with yourself in the deepest, truest way. Take some time to let this soak in, and get used to this feeling of connectedness with yourself."

Lily's mind relaxed, confident everything happening was exactly what she needed. Her mind floated in a sea of nothingness. No worries, no stress, no emotions. Nothing mattered at all. This nothingness was not cold or harsh, it was blissful and peaceful. *Oh, to be able to stay here forever ...*

Serena gently brought Lily back to the present with the quiet tones of a singing bowl. Even back from the void, she still felt a deep peace she didn't realize was possible. "This is the most amazing feeling. What just happened?"

"We connected you with your soul, and also to the divine healing energy of the earth and the heavens. Most of the time we are too preoccupied with other things to notice the soul. Our emotions, thoughts, memories, beliefs, activities, aches, pains and other sensations can keep us distracted and can block that connection. But our soul will keep trying to get our attention. Sometimes life can get pretty uncomfortable before we start paying attention."

"I've been getting more and more uncomfortable with my life lately. I have a great job as a nurse, but somehow it has been feeling meaningless and empty. It's like my life has been drained of color and is now just black and white, but I want a life that is full technicolor! I have a wonderful man in my life. I'm 33 and would love to have a family, but I'm not absolutely positive that he's the one. I really do love him, but lately I've just been feeling uncertain about everything in my life. I really have nothing to complain about, but I feel like I'm lost somehow and can't find my direction. Does that make any sense? Is that my soul trying to get my attention?" she asked, recalling the previous night's experience.

"Yes, that's exactly what is happening. The soul tries to help us make changes in our lives that are more in alignment with our purpose. When we are in alignment with our soul and our purpose, we feel fulfilled, happy, and at peace with ourselves. If you would like to continue working on this, I can teach you to tune in to your soul and find out what it is trying to tell you. It can even guide you in making positive decisions, and help you find your direction."

"That sounds perfect. I definitely want to get clarity on what to do with my life and what will make me happy. Is there anything I can do in the meantime, until I see you again?" Lily asked, anxious to get this going right away.

"Start with meditation to take time to quiet your mind, ground and center yourself, and see if you can envision that light in your center just like we did here today. Don't be frustrated if it doesn't happen as easily at home. It will get better the more often you go there and the more you practice connecting with yourself. And write in a journal every day; it will help you to gain clarity, sort out what you are thinking and feeling and allow your soul another way to speak to you. In this way, you can actually begin to have conversations with your soul."

Lily felt the truth of what Serena was saying, and even though she would like everything to be fixed immediately, she agreed that it would take some time and some practice. She set up a schedule to see Serena every other week. Helping her connect more easily with her soul, bringing to light the cause of her discontent, and hopefully healing it, would definitely be worthwhile. She promised herself she'd take time each day to follow Serena's suggestions, and wait to see what happened.

Chapter 2

My assignment is to connect with my soul and write about it, having a conversation with my soul. Sounds ridiculous, and impossible, but here goes ...

I feel so conflicted and lost in my life. I am begging for your guidance, please tell me what you want me to do.

I sit and wait for a response ... (crickets)

~Lily's journal

They had plans to go out to dinner tonight. Derrick was picking her up at six. The memories of when they met came flooding through as she was getting ready for her date.

It was over a year ago now when Lily had gone to the Landscape Arboretum on a spring afternoon to relax and enjoy the beautiful day by walking and basking in the lovely, fragrant flowers and trees in full bloom. The crabapple, cherry and plum blossoms' heavenly aromas filled the air. She liked to go there by herself, for solitude, and to de-stress. On that day, she was sitting on a rock in the Japanese garden watching birds splashing at the edge of the pond, absorbed in the moment, when a deep baritone voice spoke right behind her, from about a foot away. Startled and jolted from her reverie, her foot slipped off the rock and into the water up to her knee. He grasped her arm to keep her from falling in completely. He pulled her away from the edge. She was still shaking and trying to regain her balance when she finally looked up at him. The sun was shining behind his head, making it look like he was glowing. He was strikingly handsome, and she was frozen to her spot, not knowing what to say or do, and embarrassed by her near fall.

"I'm sorry I scared you; I thought you would have heard me walking up. I'm Derrick. Is it all right if I intrude on your private garden here?"

"Oh, it's not mine, feel free. I should probably move on anyway."

"Please stay, I'd rather not be by myself here, you never know who might sneak up behind me." He smiled a gentle, playful smile. His brown eyes showed sincerity and kindness as he winked at her.

"Alright then. I think I'll move to the other side though, where you can't knock me off my rock," she said, volleying the verbal ball right back to him. "And where my foot can dry in the sun."

He smiled, but stayed where he was, watching the water, birds, fish, and her. Eventually she got up to leave, and he caught up with her on the path. "Would you like to get some coffee? I think I owe you that much for causing you to fall in the water."

"Uh, I don't even know you. You could be a crazy person stalking me through the woods."

"Yes, I could be, but how many crazy stalkers would offer to buy you coffee? Well, maybe they would. I would just like the chance to talk to you a little more. If you still think I'm a crazy stalker after that, I promise I won't even follow you home."

She laughed despite his bad jokes. "I am thirsty. An iced tea would be really good right now. It's too warm for coffee." She normally wouldn't do this, but there was something about him, something that made her feel like she could trust him. Besides, it was just iced tea, right?

"Iced tea it is, then."

They walked to the patio together. She found a table in the sun while he went to get the drinks for the two of them. They sat and talked there most of the afternoon. Their conversation was light and easy, and felt quite comfortable. He admitted that he came there for garden ideas. He wanted to do some landscaping and gardening around his house. He was a financial planner, but liked to spend time working in his yard on the weekends as his stress relief. They talked about plants and designs. They joked and laughed about other topics as well, and had such an enjoyable afternoon, neither of them wanted it to end. Who would have guessed she would fall in love while falling in the pond?

The door buzzed, bringing Lily back to the present. Derrick came to the door, and she greeted him with a quick kiss and hug. "I'm all set, we can go now." They walked down to his car. "How was your day?"

"Nothing out of the ordinary. How was yours?"

Lily wasn't sure how much she was ready to share of her experiences of the last couple days. She wasn't sure what to think of it herself. So, she decided to keep it simple. "I went to an energy healer today. It was an amazing experience! I don't know how much I can explain of it yet, because I don't really understand it all myself. But I'll just say it was incredible."

"What made you decide to do something like that?"

"I saw an ad for it and it really spoke to me. I thought I'd give it a try, just for fun, and see what it was like. I'm so glad I did. It was one of the most unforgettable experiences of my life!"

After a long, awkward silence, she asked, "Do you have a problem with energy healing?"

"I think it's a waste of money. Most of those things are just scams to take people's money. I just don't want you to be taken advantage of."

Lily gritted her teeth, her muscles tensing. "I am 33 years old and smart enough to tell a scam from the real thing when I experience it. I'm offended that you think I can't take care of myself. I've lived alone for the past 14 years, and somehow managed to do it without being take advantage of even once, and without your help. It's a miracle I've survived so long on my own!"

"OK, let's change the subject, I don't want to fight. This is not how we want the evening to go, is it?" They rode in uncomfortable silence for a few minutes. "My parents are coming into town next weekend. Let's compare our schedules to find time to spend with them; I know they want to see you while they're here."

The rest of the evening they talked about more neutral subjects and got along just fine. He had always been protective of her, and usually it seemed chivalrous. Lily was bothered that he reacted so negatively toward her decision to go for energy healing. For some reason that felt like a big deal to her, even if she didn't quite understand why.

Chapter 3

I've listened to some meditations, and it does seem to be very effective in helping me to relax and de-stress after a busy day. It makes me much happier and calmer.

Soul, I imagine you as being the deepest part of me. Why then is it so difficult to connect with you? Maybe I'm connecting more than I know. But how will I know?

~Lily's journal

The most beautiful arrangement of flowers was delivered to the nurses' station the next day. It was a monstrous display, similar to what you'd see at a funeral, with a dozen pink roses, some small purple flowers she didn't recognize, and of course huge fragrant stargazer lilies. Everyone was ooh-ing and aah-ing over them, wondering who they were for and who sent them. "They're for Lily," the charge nurse announced.

Lily's mouth dropped, along with all of the files she'd been carrying, which scattered across the floor. "You're kidding, right? For me? I don't believe it!" It had been a long time since she'd gotten flowers and it wasn't Valentine's Day or their anniversary.

The card read, "*Just wanted to brighten up your day, I love you more than I can say! Derrick*"

Lily was very touched by this thoughtful gesture, even if it was a little over the top. She preferred simple and understated, a simple stem would have been enough for her. He had always been a romantic and liked to do nice things for her to show that he cared. She had initially been impressed by his attentiveness and thoughtfulness. But lately their relationship felt a little flat, like they'd gotten in a rut and were losing their spark. This was especially true last night after they argued about energy healing. The date pretty much lost momentum after that. Maybe he was more in tune with her than she thought, picking up on the fact that she was very disappointed by his lack of support. Maybe he was trying to make up for that now.

"So, when are you going to marry this guy? Killer looks, a real job, money, a nice house, not to mention how good he looks in a pair of jeans ... and now he sends flowers too! Doesn't get more perfect than that, girl! If you don't want him, just send him over to me." Nicki was her closest friend at the hospital. And though they didn't get together much outside of work, it was nice to have someone she could talk with during her shift. Nicki was a couple years younger and single too, but she always seemed to attract men who were trouble. Lily would love to find someone like Derrick for Nicki, though he probably wouldn't be exciting enough for her.

"I don't know. He's been hinting that he wants to settle down. I'm not sure I'm ready yet. Even though I know my clock is ticking, I want to have a family, and I love him, how do I know if he's the one?" Lily sighed, her elbow propped up on the desk and her cheek against her fist.

"I wish I knew the answer to that one. I rarely find a man I want to keep around longer than a month. They say that when it's right, you'll know. But how can you tell if that's true? Hopefully he won't ask you until you know the answer for yourself."

Changing the subject, Lily asked, "Do you know much about healing?"

"Of course, we're in a hospital."

"No, not that kind of healing. I mean, like energy healing, soul stuff."

"I don't, but I have a cousin who is a massage therapist and is into all kinds of weird new age treatments and ideas. She goes to this church in Minneapolis that has healers and psychics. She says they have classes there that people can take to learn about all these spiritual things. She's been trying to get me to go with her, but I haven't yet. I could find out where it is, in case you want to check it out."

"That would be great. I seem to be drawn to learning more about this type of healing lately. It just seems there is so much out there I don't know about that could be really helpful. And at this point in my life, I'll take all the help I can get!"

"I'll text her at lunch to ask her what the name of that place is, then we can look it up and get more information," Nicki offered, as she set off down the hall to help a patient.

Lily was excited to be getting more opportunities to explore her new fascination with the soul and healing. She was also grateful that Nicki was open to talking about it without judging her. Maybe she could talk Nicki into going to this place with her.

Following Serena's advice to do some meditation, Lily found a few places that offered meditation classes for beginners. She had no idea there were so many different types of meditation. Maybe it would be best to try a few to see what she liked and what worked for her. There was a class she could go to this evening that sounded good. Serena had also recommended a couple recordings of guided meditations that might help her as well. The nice thing about those was she could listen to them at home whenever she wanted. She would order those online when she had a chance.

The morning passed quickly, as it usually does in the busy hospital. Lily met Nicki in the cafeteria for lunch. "I contacted my cousin, Maria. She gave me the name and address of the place she attends. She says it's more of a spiritual community than a church, but they do meet every Sunday. They have a different speaker every week, and there are classes, and other events going on, too. The speaker this week is talking about 'Divine Presence in our Daily Lives,' and next week is 'The Healing Journey.' There is an energy healing class starting in two weeks,'" Nicki read the message out loud. "What do you think? Does any of this interest you?"

"Actually, it sounds exactly like what I am looking for. Could I persuade you to go with me? At least this first time? You could introduce me to your cousin," Lily pleaded, giving Nicki big, sad puppy eyes.

"Well, I am free this Sunday. I guess I could go with you this week if you want. I'll let Maria know to save us a couple of seats," Nicki agreed reluctantly as an act of friendship and support for Lily. "This will get Maria off my back about it, too. I'll be killing two birds with one stone."

"Alright, it's a date!" Lily was actually excited about this outing, which even surprised her, since it was basically church, after all. Part of her hoped it would be a lot more than that. She was starting to realize that when things lined up so easily, with all the details falling effortlessly into place, it was more than coincidence. It was an answer to a prayer. She was being helped!

Chapter 4

Even though I'm not receiving clear messages during my meditations, I am feeling a strong push, almost a compulsion, to stand up for myself, what I want and what I believe. I've never felt that before. Soul, is this your doing? Is this what you want for me?

Yes! (This yes came as a sudden unbidden thought that popped into her head.)

(Sigh) Thank you, I guess that is exactly what I need. Thanks for the boost!

~Lily's journal

L ily called Derrick as soon as she got home from work. "I had the most beautiful flowers delivered to me at work today," she said, gazing at the huge display that filled her entire table.

"Really? Should I be jealous?" he replied jokingly.

"Probably, it was a thoughtful and romantic gesture, and

the biggest arrangement I've ever seen. You could learn a lot from this guy," she teased back.

"Hmm, how can I compete with that? How about I cook you dinner tonight? Come over about seven."

"That sounds wonderful. I really didn't feel like cooking tonight anyway. Would you like me to bring anything?"

"Just your beautiful, smiling self. I'll see you then."

She hung up, smiling to herself. She loved being romanced. Who didn't? Derrick could be so thoughtful and romantic sometimes. It was one of the things she loved most about him. But delivering flowers and cooking her dinner in the same day ... something was up. She knew they were serious, but she wasn't sure if they were ready to get engaged. What would she say if he asked her tonight? She loved him, of that she was sure, but she felt so uncertain of everything else in her life. She needed a little more clarity before she made any big decisions. Hopefully he won't ask tonight. She was pretty sure he wouldn't understand her hesitation or her reasoning. She certainly didn't want to hurt him or make him feel rejected because she was confused. This was something she needed to sort through to find direction in her life, and she couldn't make any big decisions until then. She sent a prayer up, "*Please help Derrick to understand what I'm going through and be patient with me. If we are meant to be together, please help us to work it out. And if not, help me to know without a doubt what I need to do. Thank you.*"

Not knowing what to expect, Lily decided to dress up for dinner, wearing a green sundress that showed off her curves nicely and brought out the gold flecks in her eyes. "Oh, but I wanted to go to that meditation class!" Checking the listing, she found there was an early session that started in 15 minutes. If she left now she could easily go to that and still make it to Derrick's on time. Grabbing her purse and keys, she wasted no time and was immediately out the door.

The meditation class was held in a yoga studio about a mile from her apartment. It was in an old brick building, with gardens surrounding it and a courtyard in back. The yoga room was located on the main level, with hardwood floors, and some of the walls were the original brown brick. Strings of white light lined the ceiling, negating the need for overhead lighting. A small table with a lit candle sat in the middle of the studio. Other students were grabbing cushions from a stack in the corner and claiming their spots on the floor circling the candle. Lily followed their lead.

The instructor asked if anyone was there for the first time. Lily was grateful that five people raised their hands along with her. "Welcome, everyone! This is a basic class to help you to settle your mind and focus on one thing, this candle. You can sit gazing at its flame. Or you can allow your eyes to close and come back to the candle if you need to refocus. In this way, the candlelight is our tool to bring us back to the present moment. As thoughts come to you, allow them to pass by like a cloud blown on a breeze. Passively notice them come and go, with no judgment or attachment. We'll begin with a chime, and I will keep track of time and will chime again when it is time to end. We will also discuss your experience and answer questions before we leave. Any questions before we get started? OK, then let's begin."

Bong ... the chime sounded. Lily sat not really sure what she was supposed to be doing. She stared at the flame of the candle. Thoughts of her plans with Derrick, her worries a⁻

their relationship, then work, her grocery list, things she needed to do, all passed through her mind. Some of these thoughts persisted longer than others, and some kept circling. Eventually she became mesmerized by the flickering light and her mind went blank. Her breath continued to flow in and out. She blinked when necessary, but otherwise she remained still inside and out. That is, until her back started hurting and her mind started whirling again. She mentally beat herself up for not being able to maintain this state of peace and calm. The bell sounded, and she could finally move around.

The instructor reiterated, "if you experienced any sense of quieting or calming of the mind, even if it was just for a moment, that is exactly what we hoped for. And if you didn't get that, allow for it to happen as it needs to, without judgment. There is no perfect or right way to meditate. Each person is unique, with different needs. The brain and nervous system function differently for everyone. What works for one person may not have any effect at all for another. You need to find what works for you."

Lily breathed out a sigh of relief. She was sure that she had done it wrong. But after hearing this explanation, she realized she actually did do it right. She was much more peaceful than when she came in. Her stress seemed to have melted away. Nothing could bother her, she would just float on home.

Still in this relaxed state when she got into her car, she rem~   ' her dinner plans. She drove to Derrick's without
                  othered when another car cut her off, or when
                  ed at her to go after the light turned green. It

) to Derrick's door without any of the fears

she had earlier, trusting that it would all turn out perfectly. He opened the door to greet her before she reached the top step. "Wow, don't you look beautiful!" Taking a moment to appreciate her, he enjoyed the way her auburn curls floated down her back, and the way the dress accented her toned body and long legs.

Lily appreciated him right back, in his designer jeans and a plain black tee, both fitting him perfectly and showing off his runner's form nicely. He really was a good-looking man, very easy on the eyes.

"It's not every day a girl gets flowers and a home-cooked meal by a gorgeous man. I thought I should at least look nice for it." They hugged and shared a loving kiss at the doorway.

"I'm thinking I may need to do this for you more often."

"I certainly wouldn't object." The flirtatious interaction between them was a welcome change. They had both been so busy with work, and also comfortable with each other that they didn't flirt much anymore.

He led her to the living room of his spacious home. He lived in an upscale neighborhood in the suburbs, in a newer two-story home. "Can I get you something to drink? Wine? Iced tea? Sparkling water?"

"Sparkling water would be lovely. Thanks." She sat on the couch, looking around the room. It was so warm and inviting, decorated in warm colors of brown and green. It was not the typical bachelor pad. His sister had helped him decorate, and Lily loved her taste. He hadn't skimped on anything either. He made good money and liked having nice things. Nothing wrong with that.

Derrick returned with her water, and had a beer for

himself. "Thank you! So, what is on the menu for tonight?" She inquired with a whimsical air.

He proudly announced, gesturing like a maître 'd, "Tonight at Chez Derrick, the special is grilled filet mignon with sautéed portobello mushrooms, with grilled asparagus, and garlic herb biscuits on the side. Will that be acceptable to mademoiselle?"

"Mmmm! That sounds heavenly! My stomach is growling just thinking about it."

"Glad to hear it, because it is almost ready." He left through the patio doors to check the grill.

She followed him out onto the deck. It was a beautiful evening, with the sun just starting to set, streaking its stunning colors across the sky. It was the perfect background for the gorgeous landscaping Derrick had done in the yard. "It is so balmy and tranquil out tonight. Too bad we can't eat out here."

"I agree. I need to get some patio furniture. I'll put that on my to-do list. Though the mosquitos will probably be coming out soon. It's getting close to sundown, I'd hate for them to carry us away!" He filled a platter with food from the grill. The mouth-watering aroma could have all the dogs in the area swarming the yard. "Our dinner is ready, let's go in." She reached up and kissed him on the cheek as she walked by him and through the patio door.

The meal was delicious, even more scrumptious since it was planned, cooked, and served with love. After eating, they cuddled together on the couch and gazed at the fire in the gas fireplace. It was relaxing and felt so good, like she was exactly where she needed to be. Suddenly Lily had the sensation of being watched. She turned to discover Derrick staring at her intensely. "What? Why are you staring at me?"

"You are the most beautiful woman I have ever known. I know how lucky I am to be with you. I love you so much that sometimes it scares me."

"I love you too. And I'm so grateful to have you in my life as well. I guess we both appreciate what we have enough to not take it for granted."

He leaned in and kissed her softly on the lips, gently nipping at her top lip, then her bottom lip. She joined in and pulled him closer, deepening the kiss. Slowly and tenderly they expressed their love with their mouths and hands. Heat was building, as if an inner flame had just ignited and was being fanned. They teased and tasted each other, with growing intensity and enthusiasm. Somehow they ended up stretched out on the couch together, side by side. Lily reached around him and laid her head on his shoulder, a little out of breath.

"Whew! It's getting hot in here!" She turned within his arms, so that she faced the fire. Giving herself a breather, she hoped to cool off a bit.

He held her tight to his chest and continued to place sweet kisses on her head and neck. "Yes, it is, but it's not from the fireplace." His hands slowly moved along her body.

"I think I need a drink of water. Can I get you anything?" She asked, as she sat up and tried to slip out of his arms.

"No, just you. You're all I need. Hurry back!"

Lily went to the kitchen for some water and fanned herself with a plate she found on the counter. They needed to cool down, and slow down. When she was younger, she didn't have good boundaries with men. Never felt like she could say no, afraid what would happen if she did. She had had other relationships in the past that moved fast. She went along with it because she thought she was in love, and that it would last. But then when it ended, she was devastated and wished she hadn't let it go so far. The last relationship she was in lasted two years, and she was sure she was going to marry him. They had been living together for six months. One day he sent her an email saying he had met someone else and was in love. She came home to an empty apartment, since he had moved out while she was at work. He got engaged three months later, to someone else. Lily felt like a fool. Her trust was shattered, leaving her unable to trust men, and more importantly, unable to trust herself. She made a promise that the next man she gave herself to would be the one she would spend the rest of her life with. In order to not fall into the same trap as before, she was hoping to hold out until they were married, or at least engaged. On nights like this, that plan seemed almost impossible to stick with. Derrick was aware of her wishes, and didn't push her on it, which she greatly appreciated. His respect for her and his restraint showed what a great guy he really was. She sensed he was frustrated by always having to stop when things got too heated. But he never got angry about it or took his frustration out on her in any way. This made her love him all the more!

She returned to the couch with her ice water. "I should probably head home soon, I have to get up early."

"Can you just lay here with me for a while? I love to hold you in my arms."

She slid back into his arms and enjoyed gazing into the fire. She was so comfortable in his arms that she must have fallen asleep. He woke her at 1:00, saying, "I'm sorry, we both fell asleep. Do you want to sleep here or go home?"

"I'd better go home or I'll be late for work in the morning." She yawned and rubbed her tired eyes. "Thanks for a wonderful evening."

As she opened the door to leave, she kissed him goodnight. "I love you. Sleep well."

"Drive careful. I love you too. I'll talk to you tomorrow," he said as he stood in the doorway to watch her get into her car and drive away.

Chapter 5

A lightbulb just went off for me, and I realize that the times
when I am truly excited about something and everything lines
up for it to happen, this is my soul helping me and showing me
what it wants for me. Wow! Handy lesson to learn! Thank you,
soul!

~Lily's journal

L ily was waiting at the door of the church when Nicki's
black Mini Cooper sped into the lot. She was
beginning to wonder if she was being stood up, but
then again, Nicki was always fashionably late. It seemed
strange seeing her friend wearing anything but hospital
scrubs, but Nicki looked great in a classy red sundress and
black gladiator sandals. Her long dark hair was flowing down
her back in beautiful contrast to the red.

She gave Lily a hug in the entrance of the building. "I'm
so glad you made it. I'm really grateful that you would do this
with me," Lily admitted thankfully. She was also dressed up,
in a turquoise dress with dark blue flowers in a batik print.
They both enjoyed wearing colorful clothes outside of work

since they had to wear the same boring uniform, the same color every day at the hospital.

"Let's go find my cousin, Maria."

As they walked in, a woman with shorter dark hair was waving at them. She resembled Nicki, of similar height, with dark hair and big chocolate-brown eyes. Maria looked to be a little older, and a little curvier than Nicki. She came up and gave Nicki a big hug. "I'm so glad you finally came, it's good to see you! I've been trying to get Nicki to come here for years."

"This is my friend Lily, we work together. She's interested in healing, spirituality, and that kind of stuff. I told her you were too, so that's why we're here."

"Welcome, Lily! We can talk more about that after the service. Let's go sit down, I saved us seats." Maria led them to their seats and the service began.

Lily sat in complete attention, riveted by the speaker and all that she was conveying. Every word resonated within her and made so much sense to her. For the first time in her life, she was hearing a message in church that actually rang true. It was incredible! How many times had she sat through a boring church service with her parents, and felt like it was all just words, leaving her lucky to pick out one thing that she could grasp onto and take away from the time spent there? This time she was trying to soak up every word. Like her whole life she had been walking the desert and finally she'd found an oasis of the purest water. All of a sudden, it dawned on her, *This is another way that I am being helped!*

After the service ended, Nicki said she had to go. "I'll see you at work tomorrow. I'm going to have dinner at my mom's now. See ya, Maria." They all hugged, and Nicki made her exit.

Lily couldn't wait to talk with Maria. "Wow, that speaker was amazing! I felt like she was talking just to me, telling me exactly what I needed to hear!"

"I always like hearing her speak. I think she usually leads the service about once a month. And it always seems to be inspiring and enlightening. Since you liked that, you might be interested in some of the other things that go on here as well. There are meditation groups, classes and workshops, yoga, charity projects ... Oh, and since you are a nurse, there's a holistic nurses group that meets here once a month with a different topic each month, anyone can come." Maria excitedly explained much of what her community had to offer. "I'm here quite a bit, so if you ever want to meet up for an event, just let me know. I'll give you my contact information. You can call me anytime to meet here, chat, or whatever. I'm so glad Nicki brought you today!"

"I'm really glad too. It feels like this is where I'm meant to be, and like this was no coincidence, coming here or meeting you. Have you taken any classes on energy healing?" Lily asked while reaching out and touching Maria's arm in excitement.

"I have and I just love it! I mix it in with my massages now, and it has made my massages so much more powerful. My clients are amazed by the difference and the results they receive now!"

"I feel like that's something I would like to learn. I recently have been seeing an energy healer and it has truly changed my life and the way I look at everything in my life."

"Let's take a look at the events calendar, I believe there is a session coming up." Maria led Lily to a bulletin board with a huge calendar, filled with colorful items each day. "The classes and workshops are color-coded in blue. It looks like there is an Energy Healing class starting in two weeks. It is a three-day workshop, and it is fabulous! I took it last year and it really got me hooked! You'll love it!"

"That happens to be my weekend off, too. I'm just amazed by how things are lining up for me every single day! Exactly what I need, when I need it! I've never experienced this before, but now it is happening all the time. I don't understand it, but I'm so grateful."

"Has this been happening since you started working with the healer?" Maria asked, curious to hear her story.

Lily led Maria to a quiet corner where they could talk more privately. "Actually, it was before that. I hope you won't think this is crazy. One day I was feeling very lost and alone, confused about my life and what I'm doing. I found myself praying and crying, baring my soul. I heard a message come to me about not being alone and how I was being helped. Right after that I saw an ad for the healer, was completely drawn to it, and couldn't look away. I knew this was one way I was being helped, and it has continued ever since." Maria listened intently and was nodding her understanding, her eyes wide with excitement.

"That's incredible! I love hearing stories of people receiving divine guidance and immediate answers to their prayers. It's great how you are now aware of the blessings continuing to pour in when you need them! It's a sure sign that you are on the right path!"

"Do you really think so? I kept telling myself that these synchronistic events were ways that I was being helped. But now hearing you say that, it feels true. It is divine intervention." Lily felt a peaceful realization settle in around her, and she smiled to herself.

"You always have the choice whether or not to act on the opportunities that are lining up for you, but when you do, it seems like the blessings continue to come. As if you are in the flow."

"You're right, that's exactly what it's like. Have you had this happen in your life?" Lily asked, thinking she mustn't be the only one to have this happen.

"Yes, as a matter of fact, I have. When I made the decision to follow my guidance to go to massage school, I got into a similar flow. I have also noticed that when I get distracted, stop meditating and taking the time to connect with my soul, and start doing things that are not in alignment with my true self, then the flow seems to stop. Once I get back on track with what is really right for me, the divine flow starts up again." Lily listened to Maria relay her experience, sensing a kindred spirit in her.

"I would really love to get together sometime. It seems like we are on a similar path and I'd love to talk with you about some of the things that are going on with me." Exchanging phone numbers, they made plans to talk again soon.

"I can't wait to talk with you again. I'm so glad you came today. You can call or text me anytime." They hugged and walked out to their cars, both shining bright smiles and waving goodbye.

As she drove she smiled to herself. It felt so good to be in this flow. She had met someone who could be a good friend and they shared so many similar interests and experiences. *Thank you to whoever lined this up; I'm so grateful!*

Chapter 6

Now that I am paying attention, I am noticing things every day that are either signs, serendipitous events, or other ways that I am being helped. Finding perfect parking spots when I need them. Looking at something that I wanted to buy but thought it was too expensive, then the next day it was on sale for the price I was hoping to spend.

To my soul and all my other helpers ... Thank you! I am amazed by all that is happening in my life lately!

~Lily's journal

Lily suddenly remembered she was supposed to be at Derrick's to have dinner with his family since his parents were in town. She took the freeway to make better time. She would only be a little late. She loved his family! His parents had treated her like a daughter from the first time they met her. His two sisters were glad to have another girl around, and his brother joked with her about picking the wrong brother. They were easy to spend time with, and she looked forward to their family gatherings, more so than her own family's.

She walked in and Derrick greeted her with a quick kiss. "Glad you're here. I tried to call you but it went straight to voicemail." Over his shoulder, she could see his extended family gathered in the living room.

"Sorry, I went to church with Nicki this morning and didn't want my phone going off in the middle of the service."

His mother immediately greeted her with a fierce embrace. Had she not expected this, it would have knocked the wind out of her. "It's so good to see you again, dear. You look lovely as usual. I was just telling Derrick how lucky he is to have found such a wonderful young lady."

"I don't know if at 33 I still qualify for young lady status, but I appreciate the compliment."

"From where I'm standing, you certainly do." She leaned in to whisper in Lily's ear, "I hope my son doesn't wait too long to put a ring on your finger. I'd sure love to have you as a daughter-in-law!"

Lily managed an awkward smile, and simply nodded, not quite sure how to respond to that. Talk about pressure!

His sister, Anna, hooked elbows with her and led her away from her mother, and out through the patio doors. "You know she means well, but don't let her exuberance bother you."

"She doesn't bother me. She's great, but it did feel like she was cranking up the pressure. Was she doing that to Derrick too?"

"Oh yeah, full-court press! She's anxious to have grandchildren. I'm just glad he's older than I am, since he's taking the brunt of it right now." They sat out in the sun, on Derrick's new patio furniture. "Isn't this a gorgeous day? I wish we could sit here all day!"

Derrick peeked out throughout the door. "Don't get too comfortable, dinner's almost ready. You can't escape and hide out here much longer," he said, flashing them a warm smile.

Dinner was delicious, and his mother had cooked most of it. They all talked and joked during the meal and then gathered outside on the patio. The afternoon passed quickly, and soon the family said goodbye and hit the road. They were a close-knit family and usually got together once a month. His parents were retired and lived about two hours north of the city, on a lake, so they would be hosting the next gathering. Derrick's siblings all lived in the metro area, and saw each other more often.

After everyone had gone, and the kitchen was cleaned up, they sat together on a glider chair outside. Rocking with him while the sun set put her at ease as she snuggled up to him, resting her head on his shoulder. He put his arm around her and held her close. All the tension began to leave her as they rocked. What a perfect way to end the day!

"That was a fun afternoon. I'm so glad I could be here."

"I hope my mom didn't upset you with her not-so-subtle hints."

"She's very sweet. I know she is just trying to help, and she wants you to be happy." Gazing up at him, she thought he looked incredibly handsome in the waning light.

"You make me happy," he told her, the full intensity of his gaze on her eyes. "And during moments like this, holding you and watching this beautiful sunset, I want to stay like this forever. It is so absolutely perfect! This is how I want my life to be."

"We can't watch the sunset all day. This moment is perfect, and we should enjoy it while it lasts. Appreciating every moment makes for a happy life."

"I completely agree," he replied, leaning down to kiss her softly on the lips. "I am going to enjoy this moment," he murmured and kissed her again. "And the next moment, and the next. You're right. This would make a very happy life." He began to kiss her more passionately, pulling her onto his lap. Maybe they could kiss like this forever, that did sound like a happy way to live.

They had kissed for a good long while when Derrick sat up and looked at her with so much love in his eyes. "Do you work next weekend?"

"I work on Sunday, but I have Friday and Saturday off. Why?" She asked, sensing that a plan was forming in his mind as he sat there.

"I was just thinking that it would be nice for us to get away for a couple days. Maybe we could rent a cabin where we could relax, go for walks, and just spend time together. I could take Friday off and we could go after work on Thursday. What do you think?" Excitement danced in his eyes, and he looked so adorable. How could she say no?

"That does sound with wonderful. Do you think you could find a place available on such short notice?"

"I'm sure I can find something. It will help that it will be Thursday and Friday night and not Saturday. So, you're in?"

"Yes, I'd love to go!"

"I'll start looking tonight online and see what's out there. This is going to be great!" He logged onto his computer, looking like a little boy going on an adventure. He then came back and kissed her again. "I just want you to know how much I love you! And I can't wait to spend two whole days with you!" One more quick kiss and he disappeared inside the house.

Lily felt like a whirlwind had just swept her up. She and Derrick would be going away for two days and two nights. Her chest tightened. Was she ready for this? She loved spending time with him, and it would be wonderful to get away. They had never done anything like this before. It would exciting to be romanced. Most of her life was structured and dictated by her work schedule. She didn't have much time for fun or travel, though she did want more of that in her life. Maybe it would be good for them and their relationship to spend some quality time together, just the two of them.

She went inside to say goodbye to Derrick, kissing him briefly as he continued his research. "I'll let you know what I find. This is going to be amazing! I promise."

"I'm sure it will be. Good night. We'll talk tomorrow."

On the way home, she couldn't stop her thoughts from swirling around in her head. *What in the world am I getting myself into? What if this is more than a getaway for him? What does he expect from me? Am I ready for this? Please help me to know what to do.* She sent a quick prayer up to whoever was listening.

Chapter 7

Fear ... *a powerful protector, impenetrable barrier, motivating force, convincing illusion, manipulative ruler. I believe that fear has been the biggest block between me and my soul.*

I hereby pass the torch for guiding my life from fear to my soul. Thank you, Fear, for all your help through the years, but now you can retire. Sit back and watch from the sidelines. Soul, you are now in charge!

~Lily's journal

Derrick texted her the next day while she was at work to say he'd found the perfect place for their getaway. "I booked a two-bedroom cabin on a lake! Only an hour and a half away. Nothing fancy, but it should be peaceful and relaxing. Can't wait. Love you!"

Lily had an appointment with Serena after work today. Talk about good timing. She had so much to report to Serena. It had been a very eventful two weeks. *Hopefully I can get some clarity from this session today, then enjoy my time away with Derrick and not have a panic attack.*

Serena's office was tranquil and relaxing, with glowing candles and soft music playing in the background. Green plants and blooming flowers, and crystals of all sorts sat on every surface. Every detail seemed intended to promote healing and relaxation. The energy in the room was comforting and supportive, and she felt as if the session began as soon as she entered the room.

Serena looked at her kindly. "It is good to see you again. How are you?"

It was a simple question, and Lily started to say that she was good, but she began tearing up and couldn't get the words out. She took a deep breath. "I've been doing everything you suggested. I journal every day. I meditate; I found a meditation group that I like, and I also listen to some guided meditations at home. I went to a church yesterday that is a spiritual community and met some great people. They are having a healing workshop in two weeks that I signed up for. All of those things are going well, and I feel like everything is lining up for me in those areas. But I'm not so clear in my love life. Derrick has been really wonderful and attentive lately, more romantic than usual. Now he has planned for us to go away for a couple days to stay in a cabin. We leave on Thursday after work. I'm a little freaked out about that. I have a feeling that he is ready to move our relationship to the next level. I thought I was ready for that, but now everything is changing. I just want to put on the brakes. I feel like I'm in the midst of trying to figure out who I am and what I want. I'm not sure how to explain that to him. I am so glad to be here with you today!"

"I'm happy to hear that you are noticing the synch-ronicities that come when you are in alignment with your soul and the divine. And I'm glad to hear that you are taking action on the opportunities that are coming your way. You are making great progress. Have patience, the clarity you are looking for will come, especially since you are tuning in more and asking for guidance. Let's see what will come for you today." Serena gestured for lily to lie down on the massage table.

"Is it possible for the heart and the soul to want different things when it comes to love?"

"I suppose it can be perceived that way. The heart wants to love and be loved. Sometimes it is so starved for love that it will accept whatever form of love comes its way, whether it is real or not. If the heart is filled with fear or other negative emotions or beliefs, its desires can be distorted and confusing. Clearing and healing the heart will make a big difference in learning what will make it happy. The soul sees a bigger picture and wants what will be in alignment with your purpose. The soul and the heart can work together to find what will fulfill them both, which is the ultimate goal. Let's start with your heart, to see what we can heal there and then how we are guided after that."

"Sounds great!" Lily got comfortable on the massage table, covered up with a soft white blanket, feeling as if she were covered by a cloud. Lily closed her eyes as Serena lightly touched her feet.

"What is your intention for this session today? I know we just talked about it, but I would like you to state it in your own words."

Lily took a moment to gather her thoughts. "My intention is to heal my heart, and connect my heart and soul with the divine so that I may be guided and supported to make decisions that are in alignment with who I truly am on the deepest levels. I ask for clarity and wisdom to know what is right for me. I ask for healing of anything that is blocking me or getting in the way of my receiving all the good things coming my way."

Energy began surging through her entire body, from her feet through the top of her head. A tingling sensation ran through her to the tips of her fingers. This feeling was similar to her last session, but also different. The emotions she felt coming in were getting more intense. Sadness was welling up in her and tears started to fall, though she didn't know what they were about. In this moment, the reason didn't matter. The tears were gently flowing, washing away old hurts. Images and memories flashed across her awareness and disappeared in an instant. She had no attachment to them, noticing them come and go. She slipped off into the nothingness, just as she had the last time. Enjoying floating in a blissful and peaceful space, she was without any worries or stress.

At some point she found herself surrounded by light, and beings of light. Held and supported by a sense of peace all around her, she asked, *Where am I? And who are you? I feel so comfortable and loved here.* These questions she asked within her own mind.

Surprisingly the answers came through Serena, but her voice sounded different. It was quieter, more distant and monotone, yet still kind and gentle. "Your consciousness has traveled to another dimension where it can receive healing and wisdom as you requested. We are angels here to help you."

Lily found herself believing, even though it was beyond her comprehension. "How can this be?"

"Your intention combined with Serena's gifts of healing and assistance in divine connections helped us to connect with you. We are always with you, you just aren't usually aware of it." Lily felt the truth of these words, and even though she didn't quite understand how this was possible, she trusted it, since every cell in her body seemed to be drinking it in with joyful acceptance.

She was surrounded in light of many colors. The colors were constantly changing and flowing around her, swirling and blending together. It was spectacular to watch, but even more so to feel as a peacefulness filled her.

The voice switched back to that of Serena's. "Bring your awareness to your heart. Look to the very center of it. Can you sense its emotions? Allow whatever feelings are there to come to the surface." Immediately some sadness bubbled up, followed by hurt and betrayal, and then anger and loneliness, emotions stored up from her past experiences. "Ask your heart if there are any lessons to be learned from these old emotions? Anything that you need to learn from them before they can be released and healed? What does your heart have to say?"

Tears began to trickle down her face once more. "My heart says it doesn't want to be hurt again."

"Call forward any fears your heart has been holding on to."

Fear suddenly filled her chest with heaviness, making it difficult to breathe. There was so much of it. Darkness filled her with its thick density, making it impossible to move. How could all that have been hidden within her?

"How has the fear been helping you? What purpose has it been serving?"

"It has been protecting me, shielding me and guiding me, to keep me safe. It is like an armor that completely covers me." Lily's voice was barely audible, revealing what her heart was showing her.

"How does this level of protection effect your relationships?"

"It keeps people from getting too close to me, so that they can't hurt me as much."

"How much love are you able to receive with this barrier in place?"

She cried more, louder this time. "Not much love can get through. I never knew this."

"How long has this protective shield been in place?"

"Since I was a little girl, six years old. I was being babysat by the neighbor lady while my parents were working. Her son was a few years older than me. He was either mean to me, or he was overly nice, I never knew what to expect from him. Then one day he asked me to play a game in his tree fort. And he molested me. I didn't know what he was doing, but I didn't like it, and I asked him to stop but he laughed at me and said I was being a baby. He said if I didn't go along with it he would tell my parents and I would get in big trouble. I never told a soul." Lily began sobbing in a small voice that sounded like that of a small child's.

"Let her cry it out. And allow her to receive the love, acceptance, comfort, and protection that she needed back then. Feel how it would feel to receive that. What is it that she needs to feel safe?"

Lily saw an image of her little girl self, sitting on her mom's lap. "She wants to be held by her mom. Her mom says she loves her and that it was not her fault. Her mom is sorry this happened to her. She also sees angels gathering all around her, and she knows she is not alone and not abandoned. Wow, that is important to know, that even when she felt alone, she wasn't." Lily felt deep healing coming into the younger part of her that had been hurt so long ago. The weight and constriction of that pain began releasing and lifting.

"How does that feel to know that?"

"It is comforting. But it also makes me angry! If angels were always with me, why didn't they stop that from happening?"

"Ask the angels, from this connected space."

Lily was quiet for a minute. "They say they are so sorry that they couldn't stop this from happening. They wish that they could have done more, but their powers were limited. All they could do was be with me and try to comfort me. I feel their sadness and compassion. I'm still upset that it happened, but I don't blame them."

"So, in response to that incident, your body put a protective shield in place to keep you from being hurt by others. Is that right?"

"Yes, a thick heavy armor, so even if they tried to hurt me, they couldn't do as much damage."

"It was necessary to protect you at that time. You were young and vulnerable and needed the extra protection. But has it been effective in keeping you from being hurt throughout your life?"

"Not really, I still have gotten hurt. In all of the relationships I have had, I never let them get too close to me, even the people I thought I loved. I now realize that I haven't received as much love throughout my life probably because of this shield. I was also hurt from not receiving the love I craved. It really isn't helping me anymore."

"And besides keeping you from receiving love, how else is this shield effecting you?"

"It is keeping my body tight and restricted. It is limiting my breathing. It feels so heavy now. It feels like it is crushing me. Can I get rid of this shield?"

"Yes. Thank the fear for all it has done to serve you in keeping you safe all these years. Let it know that you are not that vulnerable little girl, you are stronger now and ready to do things differently. Release it with your blessings." Following Serena's guidance, the weight of fear began to lighten as she felt it slowly releasing and vaporizing, floating away to the heavens. A deep breath filled her, and she exhaled with a sigh. "Now without the fear blocking you, allow yourself to feel the love within your heart. The love you have for yourself and others. The love of the divine flowing in for you. Feel the love flowing in and out of your heart. Feel how it expands to radiate that love all around you."

Lily imagined a pink light radiating from her heart in three dimensions, creating a sphere of love all around her. It continued to expand, and she imagined her energy becoming enormous, without bounds. Her pink light was connected to all around her in love and light. Through these connections, love energy was flowing freely to her and from her to all around her.

Sighing out loud, she said, "Mmmm, this is exquisite! This is what it is all about, isn't it. If everyone in the world could experience this and connect to their love energy, what a beautiful world it would be. Maybe we really could truly live in peace." She let this wisdom penetrate into every cell.

"Now let's connect this heart and love energy with your soul and your deeper truth. First tune in to the light at your core, in the very center of you. See this light forming a column that expands vertically through your body to connect you to the earth through your feet and the heavens through the top of your head. This light is the most intense at your center, that is the seat of your soul. Take a few deep breaths and allow this light to expand to fill you and connect with you above and below." Lily breathed slowly and intentionally as instructed. "Focus your attention on the brightest point in that column. Feel the secure comfort of being held by your soul." Lily's body relaxed even more, sinking further into the massage table. "Imagine a connection between the heart and the soul. What does that look like? How does it feel?"

"It seems like there is a bridge between the two. The bridge is wide and composed of solid light, if that makes sense. At first, I thought it was made of crystal, but that was too rigid; it is more flexible and moveable than that, but it does have that look of shimmery crystal. And the feel of it ... how do you describe the feel of the deepest love and wisdom? It feels calm and crystal-clear like a mirrored lake. Warm and inviting like a cozy cabin with a fire in the hearth, comfortable and safe. There is also a peace, and a knowing that I don't have to figure everything out right now. I trust that it will come to me in the perfect timing. I really do feel safe, actually more safe and secure than I felt with the armor. I have inner strength and wisdom that I can trust to guide me."

"Take some time now to get used to the feel of this connection. Notice how strong it is, that it will not be severed. Even on days when you are not consciously aware of it, the connection will still be there. And you can tune in to it at any time. Call on it to guide you and help you to make decisions. Take a few moments to sink a little deeper and truly feel this connection, this bridge, throughout your entire being."

Lily lost track of all sense of time and space, not knowing how long she was in this peaceful state. To be fully connected to all parts of herself in this deep way, was beyond her expectation. It was truly sublime!

Selena brought her back to the present with the help of crystal singing bowls. Slowly and gently she found herself back in the room, and able to feel her arms and legs again. She had been somewhere else but had no idea where that other place was. It really didn't matter either. All of her fears and worries that were consuming her when she came in today had vanished. She continued to radiate light and love. Life appeared so amazing and wonderful!

"Thank you, Serena. That was so incredible, I don't even have words to express my gratitude. There were so many blessings in that session. I feel like I should journal right now so that I don't forget anything."

"Journaling would be a great thing to do to keep it in your awareness and let the lessons sink in even more. That was a very powerful session! The fact that so much happens for you each session shows that you are ready for more, and also that you are doing your homework and preparing for each next step. Keep up the good work!"

"Do you have any more homework for me this time?"

"Keep journaling and meditating. Pay attention to the signs and synchronicities. Enjoy that healing workshop. I can't wait to hear how that goes for you. One thing you might want to consider is having an honest talk with Derrick about what is going on with you, so that he can understand how you're feeling and that you need some time to figure out who you are and what you want."

"I agree. I know we need to have that conversation. I had been putting it off out of fear. Now I feel like I am clearer and can speak about it more openly. He may not understand, but he may at least give me some time and space to figure it out. I hope he will."

"If he loves you, he will respect whatever you need. It is up to you to speak up for yourself. Your needs are just as important as his."

"You are right. I do tend to put everyone else's needs ahead of my own. I think I'll have to make a point to change that. Thank you so much for all your help. I'm so grateful to have found you!" Lily gave Serena a heartfelt hug and wished her well. She walked out but barely felt her feet on the ground. The pervasive lightness and peace made her feel like she could fly home.

What could she do that wouldn't disrupt her peace? She pictured herself sitting against a tree in the sun with her journal. I'll go for a walk and sit in the park and journal ... what a perfect plan!

Chapter 8

I feel a connection between my heart and soul. When I was living in fear, my heart and soul were each doing their own thing and left me feeling totally conflicted. Now that they are reunited and working together, I feel at peace within myself. I am better able to trust that my answers will come in divine timing.

Heart and Soul, can you two work together, figure out what would make you both happy, and let me know what that is? (A gentle warmth filled her body, like an inner hug.)

Thank you!

~Lily's journal

L ily enjoyed the quiet sunshine in the park for about an hour. Journaling her thoughts and experiences from the healing session helped her to sort everything out in her mind. *I should discuss this with Derrick right now while it's all straight in my head, and before I talk myself out of it.*

Derrick was already home from work when she arrived.

"Hey, beautiful! What a nice surprise!" Kissing her lightly on the lips, he said, "I was just trying to figure out what to have for supper. Now that you're here, I'll make something you'd like, too."

"That's ok, whatever you were considering is fine. I wasn't expecting you to cook for me, though now that you mention it, I'm sure whatever you make will be better than what's in my fridge."

Derrick began pulling food out of the cupboards and fridge. "You really don't want the peanut butter and jelly sandwich that I would have made myself. How about stir-fry? It looks like I have everything for that."

"Perfect. What can I do to help?" She joined him in his spacious modern kitchen.

Derrick pulled vegetables out of the fridge and set them on the island in the middle of the kitchen. "Would you mind cutting up some of these veggies? I'll get the chicken started." He made quick work of thawing and cutting the chicken and throwing it into the pan.

They worked well together and had the meal ready in record time. This is what it would be like for them to be together on an everyday basis. They were certainly compatible and made a great team. Cooking a meal together seemed like the most natural thing in the world. They sat and casually talked about their day while eating the delicious chicken teriyaki stir-fry.

"So, what brought you over tonight? You have never stopped over for no reason. Not that I'm complaining, I'm always happy to see you, and love spending time with you. This is just out of character. So, what's up?"

CHAPTER EIGHT

"Well, I wanted to talk with you about some things I've been going through. I know I've been a little preoccupied lately. I wanted to make sure you knew it's not about you. I seem to be in some kind of an identity crisis. I don't really know who I am and what I want anymore. I always liked being a nurse, but lately it doesn't seem to be fulfilling for me. I'm going to sessions with a healer, which is really helping me to connect with myself so that I can discover my own direction. I guess I just wanted you to know that I'm grateful for your patience and understanding. I'm sure you're frustrated with me wanting to go so slow with our relationship. I know how lucky I am to have you in my life, but I still need to keep things slow until I figure out my direction."

Derrick listened intently. The concerned look on his face showed he was processing all that she said, and trying to put the pieces together in his mind. "Are you confused about our relationship?"

"Not really. I just wanted to be clear about where I'm at, because I'm not in a position to make any big decisions right now about anything, including us." She took a deep breath. "I know that we've both been feeling pressured by your mom lately. I felt like it was important to talk about this before we go away for the weekend, that's all."

Derrick came over and pulled Lily up to stand in front of him. He touched her cheek and jaw with his hand. "I'm sorry that you felt pressured." He paused and drew her hair behind her ear. Looking directly into her eyes, he said, "I love you, and I want to spend the rest of my life with you. Knowing that, I don't feel I need to rush, because we have all the time we need. I understand that you are not ready yet, and that's okay. I will happily wait as long as I get you in the end, and for the rest of my life." He leaned down and kissed her, the love he felt pouring out in the kiss.

She sighed in relief. "Thank you for being so patient and understanding. That means so much to me. I guess I needed to clear this up now before the weekend, in case you had other expectations or hopes for while we are away." Looking down at her hands, she spoke quietly.

"This has really been bothering you, hasn't it?" He looked at her and she nodded. He reached up and stroked her cheek with his thumb, tenderly looking into her eyes. "Please put this out of your mind. We are going away for a couple days to relax and enjoy each other's company. No pressure. No expectations. Just you and me, the lake, the sunset, the loons... no stress, no work, no worries. This is perfect timing and I for one can't wait to spend two whole days with you all to myself."

They kissed some more. "You're right, it is perfect timing. I really do need to get away. And two days with you will be heavenly! Thank you." She wrapped her arms around him for a long hug, then kissed him one more time. "I really should get going. I have laundry to do so I have something to wear while we're there."

"All you really need is a bikini, if you ask me." Giving her his charming sexy smile, he pulled her close again.

She laughed and pushed him on the chest. "Of course, you'd think that, which is why I'm not asking you. I'll see you on Thursday." One last kiss and she was out the door.

She smiled to herself, happy that she had the guts to be open with him about her feelings, and very pleased with his response. How lucky she was that he was so understanding and willing to wait for her. A man like that is a rare find! Now with all her worries put to rest, Thursday couldn't come fast enough!

Chapter 9

I was so worried about telling Derrick about my confusion.
But strangely, I felt very clear about what I needed to say. It
was important to speak my truth and for him to hear it. If I
stay connected with my heart and soul, I wonder how that
will affect our relationship. It is getting easier to connect
when I am meditating or journaling, but how do I stay
connected when I am with others?

Practice.

~Lily's journal

L
ily was flitting around her apartment aimlessly trying
to get everything packed and ready. Derrick would be
here in one hour! She was so ungrounded and easily
distracted that nothing was getting done. She started packing
clothes, remembered one thing she wanted that was in the
laundry, then went to get it and thought of her beach towel.
Where was that? She began searching for her towel, for-

getting about the laundry. By the time she got back to her suitcase, she had begun a half dozen other tasks but completed none of them. *What is wrong with me today? I need to focus, or I'll still be standing here confused when Derrick arrives, and this apartment looks like a tornado hit!*

She took a deep breath, imagining the center of her connecting down through her feet into the earth. She was grounded and rooted like a tree. In another breath she was calm, focused and ready to continue.

The practical, efficient, and organized nurse in her came to the foreground. She made a list of what she needed to bring and took the list with her so that she could add to it if she thought of something else, and still finish what she was doing. She also made a list of tasks she needed to complete before she left. Checking them off one at a time would make her feel like she was accomplishing something and also keep her accountable for getting them done. Laundry, packing, groceries, cards and games, books, bug spray, sunscreen, towels. It was challenging to guess what they might need since they had never been to this cabin before, and she wasn't sure what would be provided. Looking at all the stuff she'd packed, you'd think she were going for a month! She and Derrick had planned the menu and would be stopping at the grocery store after he picked her up. When everything was packed and piled by the door, she quickly cleaned up her mess. It is always nice to come home to a clean house. Her mom taught her that lesson and it was true. The last thing you want to do after a relaxing vacation is come home and clean house. She was just finishing up the last task on her to-do list when Derrick arrived.

He came in with his gorgeous smile blazing like the sun.

He gave her a soft kiss. "I am so ready to get away, it has been a really long week! Now the weather is gorgeous, and I get to spend two days relaxing up north with you! Life just doesn't get much better than this! I'll take these bags to the car. Are you ready?"

"Yep, this is everything! I don't think we have room for much more. I had to remind myself that we are only going for two nights and not two months. I'll lock up and meet you in the car." She took a quick look around to make sure she hadn't left anything behind and then locked the door.

The cabin was only an hour and a half away, and after an efficient stop at the grocery store, they arrived by seven o'clock. The cabin was small and appeared weathered on the outside. It could really use some TLC! It was cute though, and had large shade trees around it. They walked to the other side and saw the lake. Beautiful dark blue water with gentle waves massaged the shore. The shoreline's large rocks acted as a border, but a small section was composed of sandy beach. A hammock was hung between two trees. And a porch swing near the water facing north offered the perfect view. In the morning the sun would rise from the right, and in the evenings they would see it set on the left. Just standing there breathing the clear lake air was calming.

"We haven't even been inside yet, and I love it here already!" Lily smiled and opened her arms to the sun and breeze, soaking it all in.

"I'm so glad you like it! Let's see what the inside looks like, or we might be sleeping out here."

"Don't tempt me, that hammock looks very comfortable. I think I could easily sleep there."

Inside the cabin, it was neat and clean, but could definitely use some updating. The walnut paneling made it seem so dark, even though the windows were large. The kitchen was tiny and opened up to the dining and living area. There were two small bedrooms and one bathroom in the back of the cabin. It was quite stuffy inside with all the windows closed up tight. Lily began opening up windows to let a little breeze in to air it out.

"Like I said, it's not fancy. But it is clean and quiet. What do you think?" Derrick looked at Lily, biting his lip nervously.

Lily walked around exploring every nook and cranny. "It's wonderful! I can't believe you found this. The place could use a little love, but it really is perfect for a weekend getaway! Do they rent this out all summer?"

"Actually, the family doesn't get up here very often anymore. And they are trying to decide if they want to keep it or sell it."

"Wouldn't it be great to have a place like this that you could go to every weekend? Since it is so close to home, it wouldn't be too hard to drop in for a night and come back, or even commute to work from here." Lily couldn't contain her enthusiasm, but Derrick just smiled, his dimple showing. He came up behind her and put his arms around her.

"I thought the exact same thing." He held her a little longer, nuzzling his face into the side of her neck. "Let's get unpacked and figure out what we feel like doing for supper. We could cook something we brought, we could order a pizza, or we could go into town and eat at a restaurant."

"Now that we are here, I don't want to leave to go to a

restaurant. Either of the other two options would be fine with me." She paused, looking at the four bags of groceries and full cooler of food and drinks. "We do have plenty of food here. Let's see what we can throw together. Then we don't have to wait for pizza."

"Sounds good. What do we have that's quick and easy?"

"How about sandwiches and salads. Choose your own toppings."

"Great! Let's put them together here and take it outside to eat."

"You read my mind." Lily set out the plates and began laying out all the fixings. After they had both filled their plates, they brought them out to the picnic table out on the deck, facing the lake.

Their differences were glaringly apparent in their meal choices. Lily chose a wrap with turkey, goat cheese, spinach, tomato, and pesto. Her salad was one of spinach with vinaigrette. She grabbed a bottle of iced tea, lightly sweetened with lemon. Derrick's sandwich consisted of a long hoagie bun piled high with roast beef, ham, and turkey, cheese, lettuce, tomato, peppers, onions and mayo. He added a side of potato chips to his plate, opened a beer and took a sip. She set a container of fresh strawberries on the table between them and they both grabbed a few.

"I just can't get over how peaceful it is. I feel my stress melting away as I sit here." A loon flew overhead singing its mournful song.

"Mm, hmm. When we're done eating, let's go sit in the swing and watch the sunset."

Lily had her mouth full but nodded her agreement. There

was no hurry, sunset was still at least an hour away. She usually ate efficiently to get on to the next activity, or get her work done. Now, sitting here outside at the picnic table, she realized she didn't have any reason to gobble her food quickly. She focused on what she was eating, paying attention to the flavors, textures, and smells. A memory flashed through her mind of a talk she heard a while back about mindfulness. The speaker talked about savoring each moment, even the mundane ones, and being aware of all the sensations around you. This is what he meant, she realized as she began to savor each bite she was taking. She closed her eyes to expand her awareness and awaken her senses, taking in all the beauty around her.

"Are you okay?" Derrick looked at her with his brow furrowed in concern.

Lily laughed self-consciously and looked down at her plate. "This will probably seem weird, but I found myself wanting to enjoy being in the moment just now. Savoring each bite I was taking, sensing every taste, smell and texture. Sitting out here, I'm feeling the breeze, feeling the warmth of the sun, smelling the clean fresh scent of the lake and the trees, hearing the water, the birds, the leaves. It makes me so grateful to be here with you." Her smile shared her feeling of calmness and peace.

Derrick came over and pulled her up to stand. He looked deeply into her eyes, as if he were trying to find some illusive answer within them. "You continually surprise me. I don't know if I'll ever truly understand you, but it intrigues me and challenges me to try to figure you out." He bent down and kissed her softly. "Let's go enjoy our time together, sitting in the swing by the lake."

They sat together slowly swinging and gazing out over the lake. Lily leaned her head against Derrick's shoulder. Tension slowly drained away from her body as she relaxed into him. His put his arm around her, gently rubbing her arm and massaging her shoulder. "Be careful, you might just put me to sleep. I don't want to miss the sunset."

"Well, we can't have that. Maybe I need to find a way to keep you awake then." He smoothly pulled her onto his lap and began kissing her cheek, down to her neck and her ear. A soft moan escaped her lips and her arms tightened around his neck, pulling her closer to him.

"I think I'm awake now. But I'm still missing the sunset." She turned to focus on the horizon.

Derrick continued to distract her with kisses on her neck and ears. "I can't take the chance of you dozing off."

"Look at those colors! Isn't that the most beautiful thing you've ever seen?"

"Yes, it certainly is." Looking directly at Lily, he pulled her into him again. His lips met hers with tenderness, then deepened and intensified until their tongues were dancing. His hands moved up and down her back, holding her tightly against him.

The muscles in his shoulders, chest and upper body felt firm and solid under her hands as she let them glide over his shirt. She was still in the moment, but her awareness was now all on Derrick. The musky smell of his hair and his skin, the sweet taste of his mouth with the interesting combination of strawberries and beer. The firmness of his body, the tension of his muscles, and how he responded to her touches. Not to mention her awareness of how her body was responding to him. There was a hunger and intensity between them that was stronger today than ever before.

"We are going to miss the sunset altogether if we don't stop this," she whispered breathlessly.

He sat back, still holding her tightly, catching his breath. "I want to say, forget the sunset, it will set again tomorrow. I'd rather throw you over my shoulder and carry you into the cabin."

She giggled. "That sounds like something out of the movies."

"Better than the movies, because it's real. I love you so much I feel like I could explode." He kissed her again, then rested his forehead against hers. "I'd do anything in the world for you, you know. Even if it meant letting you go so you could be happier with someone else." His voice was quiet, and she could feel the heart-felt sincerity of his words. A wave of goosebumps spread along her skin causing her to shiver.

She laid her head against his shoulder, with her arms still wrapped around his neck. Allowing her breathing to settle and absorb all that was happening, she realized he really did love her, truly and deeply. He wouldn't intentionally hurt her or betray her. She felt safe with him. And she loved him. Sitting there in his arms watching the sunset on the lake, life just seemed so perfect. She was truly blessed and grateful!

They continued to sit quietly together, slowly rocking, after the sun had set. She must have dozed off. She woke as Derrick was carrying her into the cabin. He was such a good man! He kissed her on the forehead. "Would you like me to put you on your bed or here on the couch?" She was still a little out of it and could only muster a slight moan. He carried her in to her room, pulled back the blankets, gently laid her down on the bed and covered her up. He bent over and kissed her cheek.

She reached up and pulled him closer, hugging him around the neck. "Don't go." Lily caught Derrick off guard. "Could you stay with me and hold me for a while?"

"Sure, if that's what you want." Derrick wasn't about to say no to an invitation like that. He snuggled in next to her, with her back to his chest, and wrapped his arms around her. She was asleep in seconds. Derrick wasn't sure how long she wanted him to stay but was afraid she would wake up if he tried to extract his arms from her. He soon fell asleep as well. He was a little disoriented when he woke up at 8am but smiled as he realized his arms were still around her. This is going to be a great day!

He watched her sleep, paying attention to every detail of her while he had the chance. Amazed at how beautiful someone could be while they slept, even with her hair all messy. *How did I get so lucky?*

She began to stir. "Good morning, beautiful," he said as he was finally able to remove his arm from underneath her, shaking it to regain feeling.

"Good morning." Noticing him moving his arm around awkwardly, she added, "I'm so sorry. You must have been terribly uncomfortable. Why didn't you move?"

"I wasn't that uncomfortable. I was so happy to be with you all night, and I was afraid I would wake you if I pulled my arm out from under you. It's fine, it'll wake up in a minute." He rubbed his hands together and shook them out again. "Besides it's definitely worth it to be able to wake up next to you in the morning."

She got out of bed and looked over at him. He was still dressed in the jeans and shirt from yesterday. She was too. What a gentleman he was. She really was blessed to have found such a wonderful guy. It seemed like each day she noticed more to appreciate about him. What more could a woman want? How could she not be happy with all of this?

Chapter 10

I don't know what it is about being out in nature, in the woods or by a lake or river that helps me connect to my true essence. It seems the more I relax and enjoy my surroundings, the more my real self comes forward. Maybe it's because there aren't all the other distractions I have at home, or maybe there is just something mystical or magical in nature that makes this happen. I definitely feel parts of me emerging I haven't known since I was a little girl. I know deep within my soul, I am a nature girl. I can own that as part of who I am. I feel more like myself here than I have in years. More pieces of the puzzle seem to be revealed each day. I always did like puzzles.

Soul, please help me to live in my truth and let more of my true self out to play. Help me to continue gathering more pieces and solving the puzzle of who I truly am.

~Lily's journal

Lily insisted on making Derrick breakfast while he took a shower. She figured it was the least she could do since she slept so peacefully in his arms all night. He argued that he could help when he got out, but she wouldn't have it. The mouth-watering aroma of scrambled eggs, bacon and toast filled the cabin.

Derrick emerged from the bathroom, fully dressed in clean clothes, and drying off his head with a towel. "I hurried when I caught a whiff of the bacon. It smells delicious." They ate their breakfast in the cabin since it was a little chilly outside and the picnic table was covered with dew.

"What would you like to do today?" Lily asked, while gazing out the window at the lake, its waters calm but with a gentle breeze rippling across it. "This is a beautiful morning. The sun is shining and there is not even a single cloud in the sky."

"We could take the canoe out for a spin on the lake. We could go for a walk and explore the area. Or we could just sit and relax in the sun."

"Hmm, all good ideas, can I choose all of the above?" She gave him an excited and girlish smile.

"We can do whatever you want. We have all day." He came over and put his arms around her in a familiar embrace.

"Are there paddles for the canoe?"

"They should be here somewhere." Derrick reluctantly let her go and looked in a little closet. Behind the broom, mop and a couple fishing poles, he found the paddles. "Found them. There are life jackets here too. We should grab those to have in the boat, just in case. We can sit on them as cushions if we want. Hey, look, fishing poles. We could even go fishing."

"Uhh, maybe later."

"You don't like fishing?" Derrick asked, teasing her. "I thought you were a nature girl."

"I am a nature girl, but I don't like killing the fish. I know the meat that I eat was once a living creature, but I wasn't the one to kill it. I would prefer to enjoy watching the fish swim, and maybe throw a little food for them in the water. Besides, we already have burgers to grill for dinner, remember? We don't need fish, too."

"Okay. How about if we go for a walk first, while it's cool. Then when we get back we can pack up a picnic lunch and take it in the canoe. After canoeing, we can come back here and sit in the sun or shade and relax."

"Perfect!" She stepped outside with her arms out-stretched. "I'm trying to decide if I want to wear my swimsuit or not, since it is nice and sunny, but it's still a little chilly. I guess I'll wear it with shorts and pull a shirt over it, so I can remove a layer when it warms up."

"That sounds like a good plan. I'll do that too." They both got dressed and met up again outside.

They walked side by side on the road, looking at all the cabins, lots and woods around them. Most of the cabins were bigger than theirs, but not huge. A couple of them looked like year-round homes. They all appeared to be well-maintained, so their owners must come up regularly. They saw a few people outside and waved to greet them.

"This seems like a nice area. It's quiet, but there are people around, and they seem friendly. I like the trees around the lake. It is nicely wooded and gives privacy between the cabins."

"Yes, I like that too. And I like that it's not taken over by mansions as so many lakes are," Derrick stated, appearing deep in thought as they continued walking.

Lily also had something on her mind that she was chewing on. Finally, she just spit it out. "I should tell you, next weekend I will be attending a workshop Friday, Saturday and Sunday. It teaches about energy healing and how to do some of the techniques. I've had such amazing experiences with the healer that I've been seeing that I started researching it further. The church I went to last week with Nicki has sponsored this workshop, and her cousin highly recommended it, so I signed up. I'm really excited about it. But I was afraid to mention it, because I know you don't think much of spiritual matters."

"Well, I admit, I don't know much about healing and haven't had any experiences with it like you have, so I don't have any reason to believe in it. It seems like it would be a waste of money to me, but it is your money, you are free to waste it however you want."

Lily was hoping for a little more support from him, but he was right, it was her money and her life, she could make her own decisions about what to do with it.

"There are probably things that I do or buy that you think are a waste of money, too. Right? We don't have to agree on everything," Derrick offered as he nonchalantly took her hand in his.

"I suppose you are right. We do have our differences."

"I think part of what makes us so great together is not only our similarities, but our differences."

Lily thought about this and wondered if it was true.

"I think we are a perfect match, if you ask me." He grabbed her hand again as they walked. Their steps and swinging arms were perfectly in sync, even if their beliefs were not. Taking a leisurely but purposeful pace, they soon found themselves back at the cabin where they began.

"Do you want to go canoeing right away, or would you like to rest for a bit?" Lily plopped herself in a reclining lawn chair.

"Looks like it might take you a while to leave that chair." He winked at her from the door of the cabin.

"It is a very comfortable chair. I vote for sitting with a cold drink, and then canoeing."

Derrick brought her a cold iced tea from the fridge and found himself a comfy chair in the sun. "Ahh ... It really does feel good to just sit here in the warm sun and relax." With no pressing schedule, they took their time, then gathered all they needed for their picnic, along with life jackets and beach towels. It was a refreshing change since they were both usually driven to get things done at work and at home.

The water on the lake was still fairly calm when they launched the canoe. The light breeze was welcome since the sun was heating up as mid-day approached. They dragged the canoe out onto the shore. Derrick clumsily started placing their cargo onto the canoe and was about to step into the wobbly craft.

"Have you ever canoed before?" Lily asked him.

"No, but I've been in plenty of bigger boats, it can't be much different."

Lily looked at him from the corner of her eye and sighed.

She had done a lot of canoeing when she was younger. She had been on week-long canoe trips and knew what could go wrong if someone didn't know what they were doing. She specifically didn't want to end up being tipped over in the middle of the lake. "Okay, I'll give you a quick lesson. You hold the end of the boat between your knees to steady it while I get in. Now watch how I keep my hands on the sides and my body low as I go to the other end of the boat." She moved smoothly to the bow, sat down, and then stood up and moved back again. "There, that's how you get in without tipping the boat. Now you try."

Lily held the stern of the canoe while Derrick creeped slowly toward the bow. He was a little unsteady, but made it to his seat safely. "Now you just stay there, and I'll get in back here." She glided the boat into the water and deftly maneuvered herself into the stern seat.

"Hey, I wanted to be in the back," Derrick teased.

"Too bad, the experienced one is always in the stern to steer. Here, I'll show you few of the strokes you can do with your paddle to get the boat to move and turn the way you want it to go." She demonstrated the basic strokes and he mastered them on the first try. "Where should we go?"

He pointed to the right. "How about that way?" She guided the canoe to turn in that direction and they paddled together quietly. They traveled along in silence, the only sounds they heard were the gentle splashing of the water as their paddles moved in and out, the songs of birds, and the soft rustle of leaves in the breeze.

After about a half hour of paddling, they came to a small bay sheltered from the wind, and out of sight of other boats passing by. "Let's explore in here." Lily guided them through a narrow channel to the secluded inlet. "Oh, how lovely. We can just drift here for a while without paddling. Let's just enjoy the peacefulness." Tall reeds surrounded them on all sides, but the center of the bay remained perfectly calm and still, like a reflective mirror.

Lily removed her outer layer of clothing and leaned back to soak in the sun, hoping to get a little color on her ghostly white skin. Grateful that she had thought to put on her bathing suit earlier that morning. Derrick leaned back as well, but opted to keep his shirt on. His back was against the crossbar and his feet propped up over the end of the bow. "Yeah, this is the way to live. I could get used to this."

"You don't think you'd get bored if you didn't have a million projects going on?"

"I'm sure I could find projects to do if I wanted to, but right now I'd like more time to relax like this. How about you?"

"Oh, I could definitely live like this and not miss the craziness of work."

Derrick turned around and sat on the rail to face her, leaning forward, his elbows on his knees. "Would you like to have a place like this where we could go to on our days off? A place up here so we could get away anytime we wanted."

"Of course, that would be great."

"I was thinking, we both like the area, and it has a lot of potential, and it is the perfect distance from home. What would you think if I made the owners an offer? They were considering selling anyway." Derrick's enthusiasm could hardly be contained.

"Can you afford to buy a cabin like this, on top of your mortgage?"

"Yes, I think I can make it work, depends how much they want." He took a deep breath. "This is something I've been considering for a while. Maybe it's not possible this year or with this cabin, but I just wanted to know how you felt about it."

Lily squirmed a little in her seat. "I've always dreamed of having a cabin on a lake and spending the summers there. I can't make this decision for you, though."

"I know, but I was hoping you would weigh in on any big decisions that would affect our future. I don't want to put pressure on you, but I was hoping you'd be a part of that future with me."

"Are you trying to entice me with the lure of a cabin on a lake to get me to marry you? That's pretty sly, but I'm on to you!" She laughed and tossed a towel at him, a coy expression on her face.

"If I thought it would work, I would buy it in a heartbeat!" Derrick chuckled and stood to turn back around. At that very moment, a large heron flew out of the reeds and over their heads. Derrick looked up as it was passing overhead and was thrown off balance. A large splash and holler followed. Derrick fell backwards out of the canoe and landed in the water. Luckily Lily was sitting down and able to keep the canoe from tipping over. She couldn't keep from laughing out loud, and even though she tried to control it, she just couldn't stop laughing.

"Are you okay? I know I shouldn't laugh, but that was the funniest thing I've seen in a long time," she said, leaning over him, still giggling. He stood up and found the depth was only four feet deep. He slogged through the water to the canoe.

"You think this is funny, do you?" He reached into the canoe and lifted her, one arm under her knees and the other behind her back. He quickly tossed her into the water before she could resist and get away.

"No, no, no!" She screamed as she landed in the water. "I can't believe you just did that. And here I thought you were one of the good guys."

"Ha! Maybe it's time you got to know me a little better," Derrick joked, and splashed her with water.

"Look out, buddy, this is war!" Lily yelled as she splashed him with all her might. It was a full-on splash fest. Water was splashing between them about three feet high, such that they couldn't see each other at all.

Finally, Derrick stopped and put his hands up in surrender. "OK, OK, truce." Lily stopped as well. Then they both started laughing.

Derrick came over and picked her up again. "You're not going to throw me in the water again, are you? I'm already wet."

"I had something else in mind." He leaned his head down to kiss her, lifting her closer to him at the same time. She surrendered and put her arms around his neck and returned his kiss.

"Alright, you win," she whispered in between kisses.

Derrick trudged over to the boat and hoisted her in over the sides. He looked at the boat, trying to formulate a plan in his head for getting himself aboard without tipping the whole thing over.

"I'll try to hold the boat steady while you climb in the middle." Lily braced herself against the side rails of the canoe, ready to lean to the other side to offset his weight as he got in.

Derrick slid himself into the canoe smoothly. It helped that the boat had drifted into even shallower water. "Well, that was fun! Now let's hope the sun can dry us off."

Lily handed him a towel. "Here, this will help." He patted himself off, then decided to just take off the t-shirt and let the sun warm his skin. "Shall we head back?"

"No, hurry, it feels good here in the sun." He leaned back in the canoe to enjoy the sun on his chest and face.

His body glistened like a Greek god. He took care of his body; his muscles were well-toned and in good physical condition. She knew she needed to look away or she'd be caught staring at him. She took in the beauty of the bay around them. The trees, the grasses, the water, the birds ... It was all so peaceful. She took a deep breath and let herself relax into the boat. Feeling the slow gentle rocking of the boat on the water, hearing the soft splashes of waves against the side of the boat and the shore, along with the calls of loons, ducks and other birds around them, she could almost fall asleep.

Their canoe drifted into the reeds, startling them both. "Maybe we should head back now before we are too tired to paddle," Lily offered, picking up her paddle and steering them out of the reeds.

They paddled in a casual manner, in no rush at all. They got into a nice rhythm, in perfect sync with each other. It didn't take them long to get back to the dock.

Since they were already wet, they stepped out of the canoe into the water. Gathering their gear, they unloaded the canoe and pulled it out of the water onto shore. Lily grabbed her beach towel and spread it out onto the dock in the full sunshine. Derrick had enough sun already, so he chose to lounge in the hammock under two big trees. Lily smiled to herself, thinking this was such a spectacular afternoon. Visions floated through her mind of many such days to be spent at a cabin like this, kids splashing in the water, fishing off the dock, waterskiing, watching sunsets on the beach. Wonderful happy images of family fun outdoors. She sighed, dreaming that this could be her life. As she continued to think about the future, her chest tightened, and anxiety filled her. It would be a wonderful life, wouldn't it? Something about it didn't feel right. But what was it? Why? What was holding her back? Her mind spinning, she tried to figure it out.

Just relax and enjoy the moment. Stop worrying about the future and be in the now!

Hmm, where did that come from? She took a deep breath, and slowly exhaled, relaxing her muscles as well as her mind. Wherever the message came from, it was good advice. She set her worries and anxieties about the future aside for now. Lily sent a grateful thought to whomever was helping her, feeling a little more relaxed again. She closed her eyes and enjoyed the moment with the sun warming her back, waves splashing against the shore. Yes, this was a moment to savor!

Chapter 11

Every day I am feeling more in touch with who I am, and have an easier time quieting my mind and connecting with myself. I catch my mind spinning like a hamster wheel and can now stop myself, take a breath, and settle down. Baby steps, right? I'm extremely excited for this healing class. I feel there is something about it my soul is pulling for me to get. Is it to learn healing to help others? Is it for my own healing? Or is there something else? Soul, please help me to know what it is when I come to it. Thanks!

~Lily's journal

The weekend with Derrick was great. The time away with him was good for both of them. It felt romantic, but she was not pressured. In some ways she felt closer to him than ever before, but other aspects seemed increasingly discordant. The entire weekend was extremely relaxing, and she hadn't realized how much she needed that until she experienced it. Now that they were back, she had to work every day until the workshop on Friday. Her excitement for the workshop was building to where she could hardly sit still. She finally decided to go for a walk and sit by a stream to try to calm herself and regain her focus.

She walked to a park nearby, where along the walking path she found a secluded place to sit by herself. A big boulder at the edge of a small stream was just the right size for her to sit down on. From her perch on the rock she watched the water cascading over rocks and grasses along the edge. The water was so clear. Schools of small fish swam by in masses of fluid ease. Weeds and plants swayed along with the flow. The longer she sat there gazing into the water, all of her stress and excitement melted away. She calmed and took the opportunity to connect with her soul, her inner self. Following what she had been taught, she connected to the earth, feeling grounded and rooted like the trees nearby. She then felt that grounded steady energy from the earth coming up through her feet and the rest of her body to the center of her core. Focusing on her core, she felt her soul light getting brighter, radiating out to fill her entire body and expanding out to all around her. This brought her a deeper sense of peace, and she felt connection to all of nature around her. She breathed it in, content. She stayed there for about 45 minutes and then walked back home, taking that peace home with her.

The workshop was at the church that Nicki had taken her to a couple weeks earlier. It was a small group of about 20 people. They gathered in a room full of chairs. The instructor, Marjorie, sat on a chair in the front of the room. She was an older woman with beautiful white hair cut in a bob just above shoulder length. You could tell by looking at her face that she was a kind soul, her eyes were gentle and caring, and her smile was soft and compassionate. As she spoke, the wisdom and energy she conveyed to all in the room was profound. Even if they didn't understand a word she said, they received everything they needed just from being in the room. Her teaching style was easy to understand. She had her lessons broken up into small chunks so they could practice everything she talked about to learn it experientially. Lily appreciated that since she preferred to learn by doing.

When it was time to practice the first lesson, Marjorie asked them to find a partner, preferably someone they didn't know. Lily looked around hoping to find a good one, and locked eyes with a man on the other side of the room, who by gesturing asked her to be his partner. She smiled and nodded in agreement. He came over and introduced himself.

"Hi, I'm Frank. Thanks for agreeing to be my partner." Frank Stillman was a tall man, over six feet, with a solid, athletic build. His head was shaved bald, he sported a dark goatee, and had the most beautiful eyes of deep-chocolate brown, filled with compassion. Eyes were always something she paid attention to, and these drew her in completely. Those dark pools held unfathomable wisdom and love.

"I'm Lily, nice to meet you." As she shook his hand she felt a tingle and an awareness. This caught her off-guard. What was this about? She could hardly get herself to look away from him as Marjorie was speaking. *This is embarrassing. Why am I staring at him like this?* Not usually taken in by looks, she didn't think it was just because he was attractive. She forced herself to concentrate on what the instructor was saying. When it was about time to do the exercises, she turned back to Frank and caught him staring at her. He quickly looked down at his notes.

"OK, so do you want to go first?" Lily asked. Frank just

shrugged and nodded agreement. They went through some exercises to feel energy, first between their hands and then exploring their partner's energy field. At least there was no touching, the sensing was conducted away from the body. They both did well with these exercises and were ready to move on.

The next section was focused on hands-on healing. There were several massage tables set up at the other end of the room, so that one of the partners would lay down while the other stood at the foot end of the table. The healer put hands on the tops of the patient's feet and focused on feeling the energy running up and down the body. Lily could feel a zing of energy when her hands connected with Frank's body. Once the connection was made it quickly settled down and she felt a wave of energy moving between them. She sensed it go through his body and her own, but surprisingly it wasn't uncomfortable. It was gentle, loving, and peaceful. The longer she stayed connected, it was as though there was no separation. She couldn't tell where his body ended and hers began.

Marjorie rang a bell to indicate that it was time to switch. Lily lay down on the massage table. The sensation when Frank touched her feet was similar to what she had just experienced, except that she felt it move through her body more thoroughly. It was like getting a massage from the inside. So completely relaxing! Energy was pulsing through her body, giving her sensations she had never felt before. For a while she felt like she was levitating.

They went through a few more exercises and soon it was time for the lunch break. "So, what are you doing for lunch?" Frank asked.

"I brought a lunch. I was hoping to eat outside some-where, but I don't know where. How about you?"

"I didn't bring anything, but I was thinking of grabbing a sandwich from the deli down the street and going to a park. Would you like to join me?"

"That would be excellent. Do you mind if I ride with you, since I don't know where the park is?" Lily grabbed her lunch bag and followed him out to the parking lot. They laughed over the coincidence that he drove the exact same car as she did, in just a different color.

She waited in the car while he picked up his lunch from the deli. The park was about six blocks away. They found a lovely spot near the river to sit on the grass. They each got out their lunches. They were shocked to discover that Frank had ordered the exact same sandwich that Lily had brought from home, curry chicken salad croissant. Not the most common sandwich either, not like a PB&J or ham and cheese. They were both a little freaked out by this second coincidence. "What do you think that means?" Lily pondered out loud.

"Besides the fact that we both have good taste? Maybe it means that we are going to be good partners."

"I could already tell that." She laughed and took a bite. "So, tell me, how was that experience for you both when you were on the table and when you were the healer?"

"Well, I have taken some energy healing classes from other instructors. I am studying the many different types to compare and contrast them. I teach spirituality and philosophy in college, and I'm researching how energy healing fits in with the various spiritual teachings and beliefs.

But to answer your question, in all my studies, I have never felt the energy as powerful as I did today. I'm not sure if it's the method, the teacher, the class, or us being partners. I intend to figure this out by the end of the weekend."

"This is my first healing class, so I have nothing to compare it to, but I was blown away by how amazing that felt! I have been going to a healer, but it felt different for me today as well." Lily leaned forward slightly, to ask, "So, if it's not usually like that, what did you experience before?"

"Other times I had to really focus, and I could feel just the slightest movement, almost like I must have imagined it. I got myself to imagine a wave slowly moving in and out of the body. Another time it was more like a subtle warmth under my hands. I had a hard time knowing if I was feeling it right, questioning myself and whether I was really doing it or just making it up. My instructor said it just comes down to trust, trust in yourself, trust in your senses, and trust in your guides. That was a big lesson for me, still is, I guess."

"So where do you teach?" Lily asked, very interested in his story.

"I am a professor at Lakewood College in Duluth. I am researching the connection between spirituality and healing to maybe write a book, or at least a journal article."

After they had finished eating, they walked on the path along the river to a bridge. They stood in the middle of the bridge and watched the water flowing by. They talked easily about their lives, their experiences, their hopes and dreams. It was like they had known each other forever. When Lily talked, Frank looked directly at her, fully listening, not just with his ears, but with his entire being. She had never felt so completely heard and seen by another person. She told him things she never told anyone, it was as if there was an unspoken agreement of truth and integrity between them and she knew she could trust him completely. How could this be when she'd just met him? She really knew nothing about him, and what she did know was completely different from her life. How can two people come from such drastically different backgrounds, yet share so many similarities, and connect like this?

Even though they were given long lunch breaks, Lily and Frank barely made it back in time for the start of the afternoon session. After a short lecture, they were told to choose different partners. Lily teamed up with a woman named Corrie, who was middle-aged with short spiky dark hair. Corrie was very friendly and outgoing, and seemed like a cool big sister type. They were taught some different techniques to try with their partners. Lily had to concentrate and focus her attention to feel the energy this time. The sensation of the energy in her hands was so faint. The instructor walked past, and Lily asked if she was doing it correctly. Marjorie gave some pointers, but said she was doing it right. It was a completely different experience than she had in the morning. The same was true when she was the one on the table; she didn't feel much of anything. This must be what Frank meant when he said his other past experiences had been more subtle and hard to feel. So why was it so strong for both of them this morning?

The rest of the workshop exceeded her expectations. Her skills at feeling the energy and channeling the healing through to the patient improved greatly. By the last day, she was feeling pretty confident in her skills. She did not partner with

Frank again, but they did have lunch together each day. They had an easy way of conversing and just being together. For some reason they both felt comfortable to be themselves, like they had been friends for years. They exchanged contact information, promising to keep in touch. Frank lived a couple hours away and would be driving home right after class ended. They hugged goodbye, long and heart-felt. It was hard to say goodbye despite they're having just met.

"I don't understand this connection we have, but I'm so glad we've met," Lily said as they walked to the parking lot.

"Maybe we don't need to understand it, but be grateful for it. It is a gift. We'll talk again soon." Frank left her at her car and found his own. They both looked back and gave a slight wave.

As Lily drove away she knew deep down that meeting Frank was very important somehow. She just didn't know how or why.

Chapter 12

I met someone this weekend that I connected with in a way that I've never felt before. This was the deepest connection I've ever experienced, and it happened immediately. It seemed like our souls knew each other. I also feel like my senses are heightened, and my soul was bursting out of me like a star. Whenever he was around it seemed like my energy was supercharged. Soul, could you please tell me what this was all about?

Alright, I will keep continuing to connect with you and follow my guidance and intuition. I really want to learn to receive more clear messages from you, I'm just saying.

~Lily's journal

Unable to get Frank out of her head, two days later she finally contacted him, casually talking about the workshop and what it was like to return to the real world. They emailed almost every day. He was on break for the summer, so he had plenty of time on his hands. Lily was busy working every day for the next six to make-up for her three days off. It was always a bright spot in her day to get an email from Frank.

Frank was 40 years old, a single father of twin teenagers, a boy and a girl aged seventeen. He married his high school sweetheart when he was in college. She immediately became pregnant with the twins. Maybe it was the stress of having two babies, or maybe the reality of life had revealed to them things they had been blind to before. They fought constantly and nothing he did seemed to make her happy, but they stuck it out. When the babies were two years old he found out she had been having an ongoing affair with a neighbor. That was it for him. She moved out. They had shared custody of the kids ever since. For the most part they were civil with each other and did a good job of co-parenting the children. Frank occasionally went out on dates, but never longer than a few weeks. He had no interest in being in a relationship again. That betrayal by his wife had scarred him deeply.

Two weeks after the class, they decided to talk on the phone, since it seemed they had more to say than could be easily conveyed by email. Frank called her one evening. They talked about their lives, but also about deep spiritual subjects. Frank had a way of asking questions that really made her think, and in a way that she had never thought before.

"I could ask you about the meaning of life, but how about love?" He asked.

"Well, since love probably is the meaning of life, they really are the same question, aren't they? That's a hard one; I'm not sure how to answer that." She took some time to formulate an answer. "Love is a feeling. It's an action, acting in a caring and compassionate way. It's a way of being, of radiating light and kindness. It is a connection with someone. There is physical love, sexuality. There is the idea of love, which is created by the mind. There is emotional love, which is romantic and ruled by the heart. And I believe there is soul love. I have often wondered what it would be like to have them all combine. If I am being completely honest with myself, that is the kind of love I've been searching for. I believe it's possible. What do you think?"

"I agree, that would be the ultimate goal. I've never seen it either. But I do believe it's possible, if people can heal the issues that keep them from finding it."

"Do you have issues like that?" She asked, in hopes of prompting him to share a little deeper about himself.

"We all have issues. But yes, I admit that I have trust issues that keep me from experiencing real love. It is something that I continue to work on."

"I have trust issues as well. Another thing we have in common. So, what is love to you?"

"I wish we had more than one word for this. Other cultures and languages do have multiple words for the various types of love, but in English we only have one. The word Love has so many different definitions and can mean different things to everyone. Even as far as love being something you feel for another, there are as many different kinds of love as there are people. One person may say they love you and they have their own sense of what that means, but to the person receiving that declaration, it may mean something completely different based on their beliefs, perceptions, feelings, and past experiences. In the human experience it is so complicated, when at the core of it love is the simplest concept of all. Love is the basic essence of all life. It is also the most powerful force in the universe. It can bind us together or tear us apart. It can heal all wounds or cause excruciating pain." Frank chuckled. "I'm sorry, that was the professor in me coming out. I could go on for hours if you let me. Back to your question, personally, I believe that real love is honoring and respecting a person when you see them as they truly are, flaws and all, without distortions or masks, and you accept them for all that they are on every level and connect with them deeply on all those levels as well, body, mind, heart and soul. I do hope to experience that one day."

"Did you love your ex?" Lily asked quietly, before she could stop herself.

"I certainly thought I did at the time, in that naive, innocent way that first love appears. I thought she hung the moon. Now I think it was probably more hormones than anything else. We were not compatible, not in our personalities or our beliefs. We had nothing in common but our attraction for each other. We did create a couple of truly amazing kids, and that is the real gift in all of it, the real reason we were brought together. I have no regrets. And I do still love her and care about her, but not in a romantic way. She is the mother of my children and will always have a special honor for me, but the feelings I used to feel for her have forever changed." He was speaking from the heart, but there was no sadness in his voice, just honest truth. He wasn't holding back or filtering what he said, which Lily appreciated and admired.

"Thank you for sharing all that. I didn't mean to pry."

"No apology needed, we are friends, and this is how we learn about each other and establish a level of trust. How about your boyfriend, Derrick? How do you describe that love?"

"That is a very good question, one I've been trying to figure out the past few months. He is a good man, everything I always wanted, and there's a lot of physical attraction, we get along well, but lately something seems to be off. Like something important is missing. It's driving me crazy. I'm not sure what to do about it."

"I truly believe that as you continue to connect deeply with yourself, you will get your answers when you are ready to hear them."

"Okay, I have another question for you. How would you describe or explain this connection we seem to have, when we just met?" Lily challenged.

"Do you know much about past lives?"

"Not really, why?"

"I believe that when people meet, and they feel like they've known each other forever, and they just click, it's because they were together in a past life. I have studied this some, and I believe that many of the people we have in our lives currently, have also been with us in past lives, but not in the same roles. In one life you have a husband, in the next life that soul might be your daughter, in another life they may be your arch-nemesis. I don't know what we were to each other in the past, but I do think we have known each other before."

"I thought it was just soul mates who did that."

"No, we have souls that come into each life to serve different purposes. For example, a spouse from a previous life may come into this life as a friend to support us through a difficult time. When that time passes, they may drift out of our lives again. Sometimes they are here to complete unfinished business from the previous life, to clear the karma. You might want to try having a past life regression to get some clarity about some of this and how it is playing out in your life now."

"Do you believe in soul mates?"

"I do believe in them, but I don't believe there is only one for each person. I think our souls have many soul mates, and they each serve different purposes in our soul's development. At different times in our lives different soul mates may come to our awareness as a vibrational match. The vibration may change in time, and they may end up going their separate ways again."

"That definition sure sucks the romance right out of it. It sounds kind of jaded too, if you ask me."

"I don't mean for it to sound negative, and I like romance and happy endings just as much as anyone else. I just think people put too much stock in the soul mate idea, wanting perfection in a relationship without having to work at it. That said, I do believe that people can be drawn together by past life connection, connect on all levels, including spiritually and vibrationally, and share a love that is so pure and true that nothing can touch it. I believe it is possible. It just seems to be pretty rare."

"I too believe it is out there. The problem is knowing whether to hold out for it to find you, or find happiness when you can and hope that the real thing doesn't come along after you are already married to someone else."

"That is quite a conundrum." He laughed. The gentle sound of his laughter put her at ease once again.

They finally said goodbye after two hours of easy conversation. Lily sat there contemplating all that they discussed. Was he her soul mate, or just a strong soul connection from the past? And what was their past connection? Would she ever know the answer to that?

Chapter 13

I was talking with Frank about deep soul love. I really do believe it exists. I feel a longing within me to find it. Like it is calling to me. Is that crazy? Could I be blocking myself from love that is in front of me by seeking only the rarest jewel? Missing out on happiness because I'm holding out for the miracle? Soul, please help me.

Listen deeply. Be patient. It will become clear.

Thank you! I hope you will give me clear signs or messages so that I will know what decisions are right for me. A banner across the sky would be helpful!

~Lily's journal

Derrick invited Lily to go to a play on Friday night. One of his clients had given him free tickets. It was a Broadway musical, now playing in Minneapolis, and apparently these tickets were in high demand. They were going to have dinner downtown at a restaurant near the theater first and then walk to the show. It was a beautiful evening.

Lily looked amazing in an elegant sleeveless dress that was chocolate brown, bringing out a golden color in her hazel eyes. Derrick had dressed up as well, wearing a dark blue dress shirt and a tie that was a shimmery silver with blue dots. Seeing him like this reminded her of how lucky she was to have him. How could this gorgeous man be with her? She looped her hand through the crook of his elbow, holding onto him as they walked from the parking ramp to the restaurant.

The restaurant was busy but not overly crowded. It was good that they came before the show and not after, when the rush crowd would be there. The food was incredible! Lily savored her seared scallops, stir-fry vegetables with coconut curry sauce over rice. Derrick enjoyed walleye, green beans with garlic mashed potatoes.

"I got some interesting information today," Derrick said, as they were finishing their food.

"Information about what?"

"I talked to the people who own the cabin where we stayed. Apparently, the husband has been having some health issues recently, so the wife said they have decided they will definitely sell." Derrick tried to present this as if it was no big deal, but Lily could hear the excitement in his voice and on his face.

"Did she tell you what they want for it?"

"Yes, and they haven't listed it with a realtor yet. She was hoping that if we want it, we can negotiate between ourselves and not have to pay realtors."

"So ... what do you think? Is the price what you were hoping for?" Lily asked impatiently. She put down her fork and was focused completely on the conversation.

Derrick took another bite, trying to keep her in suspense. "I think the price is fair, and they seem to be pretty reasonable people, so I'm sure we can work out a good deal for all of us. They'll even let us have any of the furnishings we want."

"So, you're going to buy it?"

"What do you think we should do?" Derrick asked, trying to involve her in the decision.

"Well, I'd say yes, if the price is good, and you can afford it. It's a good investment, the price of lake property will only go up, and it will always be easy to resell for a profit if you decide you don't want it down the road. I think it's a smart move."

"The owners want to sell it to a family that will keep it in the family for years to come, and that's what I want too. I'd like to bring our kids there every summer, and then our grandkids, and maybe even retire there someday. I just want to know if you could envision that as well." He looked her right in the eye, and she could see all the love in his vision for the future as well as here and now.

"I love that vision. Summers or weekends at a lake, who wouldn't want that?"

He reached across the table and held her hand. "I want to be very clear. I want you to be a part of that vision with me. I want that to be our future. This isn't a proposal, but I want to make sure you understand exactly what I'm planning for here. The reason I'm asking for your opinion is because I want that to be our place. Yours and mine."

Lily swallowed hard, her mouth suddenly dry as she began to comprehend what he was saying. *What do I say to that? He's asking for a commitment here. I love him, and this vision is exactly what I have dreamed about my whole life. So why does this seem like such a big step? He said this wasn't a proposal, but he's asking for just as great a commitment, isn't he?*

"I'm sorry, I didn't mean to put you on the spot like this." He sat up and let go of her hands.

"I'm not sure what you want me to say. You say this isn't a proposal, but it seems like you want a commitment from me. And I've told you many times that I'm not ready for that yet. The fact is, we are not married or engaged, so this decision is ultimately all yours. Would you be happy to have this for your future family, even if it wasn't with me?"

"Are you saying you don't see a future for us?" Derrick asked her, a little defensive, his anger and frustration starting to build.

"No, I'm not saying that at all."

"You know, sometimes I get the feeling that you're just biding your time with me, waiting until something better comes along. Is that why you keep me at arm's length? And why won't you talk about the future? I know I said I'd wait for you, no matter how long it takes. But I also don't want to waste this time if you can't see or envision a future with me."

Tears began to fill Lily's eyes. "I definitely don't want to waste your time, if that's what you think I'm doing. I would think by now you would know me better than that." Her head bowed down, tears trickled down her face. "Excuse me." She got up and escaped into the restroom. She was able to take a few deep breaths and pull herself together.

She took a moment to consult her soul. *Soul, please help me to see the bigger picture, beyond our emotions and drama.*

What is really going on here? She suddenly realized that Derrick was afraid of losing her. And she was afraid to make a commitment when she still had so many questions about her life. How could they bridge that gap? Patience and understanding. She took a few more calming breaths, fixed her hair and makeup, and was ready to go back.

Lily returned to the table where Derrick was waiting with a worried look on his face. She took another deep breath, connecting with her own inner strength. "It seems we both need to set our emotions aside. This is not a good time to react in fear or anger, or we will both regret it. Let's back up a bit." She looked him directly in the eye so he would know the truth of what she was saying. "I am not playing games with you. And I certainly don't want to waste your time or mine if this isn't right. Look in my eyes and feel my love and my sincerity. As I told you before, I am just not able make any big decisions right now until I get some things figured out for myself first. No amount of pressuring from you will make that happen any faster. I can definitely envision having a family in that cabin. But that is a vision, not a promise or a guarantee. I'm just making sure that this decision is not all about me. Would you still want it if I wasn't here? If it were just you making this decision for yourself, would you still want to buy it?" Lily asked, calmly and patiently.

"I have a hard time with that because all of my visions for the future have you in them. But yes, if it were just me alone, I think I would still want to buy this place for myself and for my future family." He breathed a sign of resignation.

"Good, then you should definitely buy it! Congratulations!" She reached across the table to hold his hand.

"I don't know if I will ever understand how your mind

works, but I still love you."

"I challenge you to think differently, that's one of the things you love about me."

"You definitely challenge me, that's for sure! In more ways than one." Derrick flashed her his flirty smirk. She gasped dramatically and tossed her napkin at him, feigning distress. They both laughed, and enjoyed a lighter, more jovial conversation as they left the restaurant and walked to the theater.

The play was fantastic. It was easy to see why the tickets were in such high demand. The both enjoyed it immensely. Derrick had his arm around her the entire show, and at first it felt awkward after their argument, but as the show progressed she was able to soften into him. At one point she felt him staring at her, and when she looked up, he met her with his lips. She loved his kisses, but she pulled away and elbowed him to watch the show.

After the show ended, they began walking toward their car, which was a few blocks away. Suddenly Derrick pulled her into the receded doorway of a building, pushed her up against the wall and kissed her hard. There was so much passion in his kiss, she had never seen this in him before. When they finally came up for air, she was breathing heavy and felt a little light-headed. "Wow, where did that come from?" She asked.

"I think It's been building up all night, I just couldn't hold back anymore. I definitely don't want to lose you. I'll admit, I was a little scared at dinner when you left the table that you would come back and say we were through. I'll do whatever it takes for us to be together. Whatever will make you happy."

He kissed her again softly. "I meant to tell you earlier that you look absolutely stunning. You take my breath away." He put his arm around her and they continued walking down the sidewalk toward the ramp.

"Then we're even, you definitely took my breath away back there." She nudged him, and he laughed along with her.

"There's more where that came from." He gave her a sideways glance. She could see the dimple show on the side of his face that was visible to her. That dimple always got to her.

She couldn't deny that they had great chemistry together. Tonight, that chemistry was exploding. Her confusion continued to grow. Their relationship seemed to be running hot and cold lately. They had fought at dinner and she was hurt by what he had said, but later he had been romantic and passionate. Her body seemed to be betraying her, even when she was angry with him, his kisses could obliterate all sensible thoughts and make her forget she was mad at him. She was completely off balance, and didn't know how she felt. This passionate side of Derrick was hard to resist, but she couldn't ignore the other side that had them arguing and upset.

She understood Derrick's impatience and his need for a commitment from her. He was a few years older than she was and anxious to start a family. She just wasn't ready for that yet. It was not that she didn't want to get married and have kids. She truly did want that someday. Someday. What if she took too long and didn't get her life figured out until it was too late, eventually deciding that she really did want a life with Derrick after he has already moved on. On the flip side, if she went ahead and married him when it was not what she truly wanted, they could have a miserable life or a disastrous marriage. Help!

Chapter 14

I've noticed that my mind gets carried away with worrying about things. This is nothing new, but I realize that I spend a lot time worrying about what I can't change, or what hasn't happened yet. I've found that when I am aware of doing this, I can stop and choose differently. I can choose not to worry about this. I can choose to think differently. I can choose to focus on what I can change. It does make a difference. What do you think, Soul?

You are making great progress. Without all the worry, you are at peace, you are more centered and connected, you make decisions that are more in alignment with your truth. Keep it up!

I believe I am opening up to feel not only my soul but other beings around me. I think there are angels around me that have been helping me. I have a sense that they are my helpers to get things lined up, or to give me a quick message in my mind, but that could be my soul giving me messages as well. I still don't know how to tell the difference between my soul and my angels. It would be nice to know who is helping me. Please identify yourself next time, so I can thank you properly.

~Lily's journal

Sitting by candlelight and writing in her journal was becoming one of her favorite daily routines. Writing seemed to help her to clear away what had happened during the day. After she wrote about it, she was able to let it go and not think about it. She didn't lie awake at night with thoughts swirling through her head like she used to. Journaling also helped her to work through some of the issues she was struggling with. She not only wrote about the problem, but asked questions. Sometimes the answers came automatically, as if from somewhere else. From her soul, or angels, perhaps? Other times she intentionally connected with her soul to ask for guidance, and then she wrote about what she felt, sensed, or thought.

It had been a couple weeks since her last session with Serena, but it felt like a lifetime. So much had happened in this short amount of time. Lily didn't know where to start, or how much of her story to share. *"Just share what is most important,"* was the message she received in her mind.

Serena gave Lily a big hug upon entering the room. Then she stood back and looked at her rather intensely. "You have had some major shifts since the last time you were here. Your energy is different and your light is shining much brighter."

Lily smiled, delighted to hear that someone noticed the change she felt within herself. It was validating and reassuring. "Thank you for noticing. Yes, a lot has happened, and I know that I am changing. I feel like I am seeing things differently, reacting differently, and I feel more in tune with myself. I took a healing class, and that was extremely helpful for me. Not only to bring more understanding to some of my issues, but I realized that there is something about healing work that really draws me in. I want to do more of that."

"Wonderful! It seems like connecting to the healer within you is helping your light to shine. What do you think?"

"Yes, I do feel lit up since I took that class." Looking down at her hands briefly, to find the words she wanted to say, she said, "There's something else that happened at that class."

Serena listened as she watched her with full awareness, assessing Lily's energy, aura, and picking up any intuitive guidance that might help her. "I'm listening."

"I met a man in the class. From the moment I looked at him, I could feel this intense connection. When he shook my hand, there was a surge of energy between us. This sounds strange, but it was as if I recognized him, even though I had never seen him before in my life. Talking to him is the most comfortable thing in the world. We can talk for hours, and share many of the same interests." She took a deep breath and let it out as a quiet sigh. "Ok, I admit that I am confused by him. I am in love with Derrick and I'm sure we would have a good life together. But now I meet this other man I feel such a strong and deep connection with, a connection I don't have with Derrick. I don't know what to think of this. I don't know if we were brought together for a reason; well, of course we were. But what is the reason? Am I supposed to be with him?"

"Phew, that is a lot to digest and sort through, isn't it? I have a feeling that much of this will unfold as you go along, and will become clearer to you as you get to know this man a little better, and also get more adept at listening to the guidance of your soul, your heart and your spirit guides. It would be a disservice for me to tell you what to do. This is the perfect opportunity for you to connect with your soul, your heart, and your guides to find your path and make choices from there."

"He said we probably have a past life connection. What do you think of that?"

"I agree. Usually when we meet someone, and we feel like we 'recognize' them, it is their soul that we recognize. We know their soul from other lifetimes when we were with them. As you know, our body only lasts for one lifetime, then the soul moves on and reincarnates in another body the next life. We might not recognize them by their physical body, they may not be the same gender, race, age, or role. But the soul is always the same throughout all lifetimes, and we can recognize it by its vibration, its light, and its feel. Have you ever had a dream that you knew was about a person in your life, but it didn't look like them at all? You still knew it was them."

"Yes, I have had dreams like that. Last week I had one about a friend from high school, Sarah. She was tall and had long, straight blond hair when I knew her, but in my dream she was a short, stocky woman with freckles and red, curly hair. Somehow, I still knew it was the same Sarah. I just thought it was a weird dream."

"I don't know what your dream was about, but it illustrates my point of how we can recognize someone even if we've never physically seen them before." Serena paused for a moment, waiting for guidance on what to say next. "Having a soul connection with someone doesn't necessarily mean they are your soul mate, or that you are meant to be together. There are many different reasons for souls to come together again. Keep working on your connection with your soul and your angels for guidance to discover what the reason might be in this lifetime. Just be open to what comes to you, if it is right for you to know. No matter what the reason is, this is a gift! Accept it for whatever it brings for you."

"That makes a lot of sense. Thank you." Lily moved over to the massage table. "I have been working on connecting with my soul, but I haven't done much with angels or other beings. Can we do a little with that, so that I know what that feels like and how to know the difference? I would like more clarity, and also trust. I would like to be able to trust myself more, then maybe I will be able to trust others as well."

"That is a very good intention." Serena made her connection with Lily by softly placing her hands on Lily's shoulders, as Lily lay face up on the massage table. She began to say a prayer to protect this sacred space, calling in all beings of light who were to assist in the healing, asking all angels to gather around Lily to support her intention.

Lily could feel the energy moving through her, first tingly where Serena's hands rested, then she felt different places in her body start to warm up. Her hands became hot. The energy was moving through her, stirring up different feelings as it moved. She felt some anxiety bubble up in her chest. It became intense and uncomfortable, like a heavy weight was sitting on her chest, making it difficult to take a breath. Then all at once it lifted, the weight became light and the fear dissipated. She took a deep breath, feeling her chest open fully. Light filled her, and she noticed the color green all around her. Other colors started swirling around her, like a psychedelic painting of brilliant color but with no form.

She felt herself floating weightlessly, with no thoughts, no sounds, no feelings, just limitless peace. It was complete bliss! She was completely in this moment, nothing else existed. This emptiness was not lonely though, in fact, the longer she stayed there, she felt the presence of loving beings surrounding her. They felt like home to her.

"I'm so glad you're here with me. Can you make yourselves visible to me?" She asked within her mind, hoping to get some idea who was with her. She could see some of the colors around her becoming more concentrated to resemble beings. Each was a different color of light, but without form or distinguishable features. "Who are you?" A response came to her mind as a knowing. Angels. These were angels around her. "Could one of you come forward and tell me your name?" She felt a green one come to her awareness right in front of her. The energy felt male, and the name that came to her very strongly was Raphael. Lily repeated this to Serena.

"That's right, Raphael is an archangel of healing. And he is known for his green aura. He is the one that has been leading this session today, bringing the light energy through me for what you needed. Ask him if he has any messages for you right now."

Lily asked the question in her mind, and spoke the answer out loud. "Feel these angels all around you now. Feel the vibration, the light, the love that we bring to you. We are always with you. Take some time to know what we feel like. This is one way that you can know who is with you, by how we feel to your body. We each have a different vibration. You can call on us anytime, talk to us, ask us for help. We'll help however we can, but always know that even if we can't help in the way that you ask, we are always with you and are doing all that we can to assist you. We love you very much. Feel our love." She felt an intense sensation radiating into her chest. A tear escaped from her eye as she felt the overwhelming love from them. She had never felt anything like this. The love from them was so pure, had no strings or conditions, and it just kept coming, endlessly. Seeing all aspects of her, even the parts she tried to keep hidden, they saw it all and loved and accepted her completely. All she could manage to say was, "Thank you."

She lay still, soaking in the love and the peace all around her and within her. Her body was completely relaxed. In fact, it was difficult to tell if she even had a body. I could just stay like this all day!

Serena began softly and gently to cue her to come back to her body and be present to the room once again. Even as the energy began to fade, she still held the love, light, and deep peace within her. Another incredible gift!

"That was amazing! I truly sensed the angels and felt them with me. They are still with me. I will continue to practice this, connecting with them and asking them to help me. When I felt all the love coming from them, I realized that if they have such love and acceptance of me, I must be all right! I knew without a doubt they spoke the truth and I could trust them. This feels like a big step for me, and important at this point."

"The more you practice connecting with them, asking for help and paying attention to the ways that they answer your requests, the easier it will be to trust. You are right when you say trust is a big issue for you. Start by trusting them, then yourself, and that will spread to others. But start with small steps; a daily practice of connecting with your angels is perfect for right now."

"I can do that. Thank you for opening this up for me. I feel like flying, I'm so light. Maybe the angels will fly me home!" Lily laughed.

Serena chuckled with her. "You're very welcome. But it is important you acknowledge that you did most of the work. This is all within you. I just helped it come forward. All the homework you do makes a difference, too. Keep up the good work, and enjoy your daily practices! I can't wait to hear what you will report next time!" Serena gave her a hug goodbye.

One the way home, she pondered all that she had experienced in that session. It was so comforting to know that she was not alone. Were these angels the ones that had been lining things up for her the last month or so? It seemed so. And with all these synchronicities, she had to trust that everything would work out for the best. It was a very freeing realization, not having to worry or try to figure everything out. She surrendered her worries to the angels and trusting them, she took a deep breath and let out a sigh to clear it all out. *We'll do this together, won't we?* For the first time in years, she felt truly hopeful.

Chapter 15

> *My connection with angels is getting stronger and I am able to trust it more fully. I find myself asking them to help me to find a parking spot, help me to find my keys, help me to choose what to buy in the store. It seems that the more I am able to trust them, the more I am trusting myself as well. I am still connecting with my soul each day, but knowing what my soul wants is still confusing for me. Soul, please help me to find a way to understand what you want more easily and clearly. Thanks!*
>
>
>
> *~Lily's journal*

Lily had been so enthused by the healing class, but now in the weeks after it, she felt the spark beginning to fade, since she didn't have anyone to practice with. This wasn't something she could do at work since people in the hospital would think she was crazy, or worse, that it was voodoo. Derrick said he accepted her doing it, even if he didn't understand. The fact that he didn't believe in it at all left a gap between them, which worried her. He did let her practice on him once, and she appreciated that. But he didn't feel a thing, so she wasn't sure she was even doing it right. The experience left her feeling even more doubts about her skills, abilities, and senses.

She mentioned this to Frank as they spoke on the phone. "Do you get to practice healing on anyone?"

"I do have a few people that have asked me to help them with healing—some colleagues, some former students. Makes for a nice side gig. I also use it with some members of my family. But I don't have anybody that does it on me, and I could really use some myself."

"Too bad we don't live closer, I would love to practice on you."

"We could do it long distance over the phone."

"What? Are you serious? Is that possible?" Lily was surprised, but her mind immediately began spinning over the possibilities this presented.

"Yes, it absolutely is. This is energy healing we're talking about, right? And energy is not limited by time and space. Energy is everywhere and everything. You could connect with my energy right now and feel it just as if we were together. It does take more focus, concentration, and openness to all sensing and feeling, and especially trust. You must trust and believe that this is possible. Trust in me and trust in yourself."

"You know I trust you. Would you be willing to try it on me so I can feel it and experience it firsthand, to see what it's like?"

"Of course. How about right now? Find into a comfortable position, either sitting or lying down."

"I'm on the couch already, so I'll just lay here. Okay, I'm

ready."

Frank's voice softened. "Take a deep breath and settle in. I'm setting an intention to create a safe and sacred space for this healing. I ask that only light and love be allowed, and that we both be guided by divine beings of light, receiving any wisdom, messages, sensations or insight for this healing, teaching, and experience for our greatest and highest good." Frank held his hands out in front of him as if they were on Lily's shoulders, like they were when they were in the class and she lay on a massage table. He imagined connecting with her energy and opening up to the flow of universal divine energy through him into her.

As Lily lay on her couch almost 200 miles away from Frank, she began to feel a tingling moving from her head and shoulders and spreading through the rest of her body. The energy was strong, powerful, gentle and loving, all at the same time. It really was just like she experienced when they were partners in the class. "Wow, this is unbelievable! I feel this in my body, just as if you are here in the room with me."

"I'm feeling some emotion building up in your chest."

"Yes, I feel some fear and anxiety coming up."

"Let's stay with that. See if any images or messages come to you as we connect to that fear. Just stay open and let it come."

"An image, like a short movie, just flashed through my mind. It was of a witch being burned at the stake, then it switched to a woman being stoned." She continued to allow it to flow through her. "They were both attacked and killed for who they were, because they were different from others. They stood up for their beliefs and for who and what they were and they paid the price." The fear continued to build in her chest. She gasped. "My fear is of what will happen, what will people do when they find out who and what I truly am. After what happened those other times, I have kept my gifts hidden to keep me safe." Lily spoke in a soft, far-away voice, not her usual speaking voice. These answers were coming from someplace deep within her.

"How is keeping your true self hidden working?"

"I feel safe."

"What does your soul have to say about this?"

Lily was silent for a few moments, as she connected with her soul for deeper truths. Tears streamed down her face. "My soul says that keeping myself hidden is living a lie. It is not happy living this way. It wants to be free, it wants to soar."

"Does your soul hold fear?"

"No, the fear is not in my soul. The fear is held in my body and my mind. My soul wants to be free of it. The fear is like a prison for my soul. I want my soul to be free." As she said those words, a flood of light came in, filling her, as lasers sliced through the bars and shackles that held her in fear. A powerful affirmation exploded from her chest, "I will no longer be a prisoner to fear!" With that the fear was blasted from her and vaporized. She was now radiating light all around her. The feelings of love and healing intensified. Her body buzzed with a pleasant vibration.

They were both silent for quite a while as Lily took in all the blessings from this healing, letting it sink deeply into her entire being. Frank could still sense that she was in a deep space of healing and he respected the need to keep it sacred by maintaining silence. He would wait until either the energy shifted or she spoke to him.

It actually happened simultaneously; the intensity lessened, and he came out of what was a trance-like experience for him that he had never experienced before. He had been feeling and experiencing everything Lily had voiced, even before she spoke about it. As he came out of it, so did Lily. She yawned and said, "Oh my gosh, I don't know if I can even speak right now. Talk about intense! I think my circuits are blown!"

Frank chuckled. "I know what you mean. I think mine might be too."

"So have you had this experience before?"

"I have done some remote healing over the phone, but never experienced anything as powerful as this. I believe I was receiving the same healing that you were. It was at work on both of us at the same time. I didn't have the same images, but they do have a similar theme, of letting go of fear and trusting who I am, who I am meant to be."

"Why do you think it was so intense this time?"

"I think there is something about our connection. It seems to me that when we bring our energies together to join in a shared purpose, it is amplified. Not like the usual 1+1=2, it is more like 1+1=infinity. I'm not sure what to make of that, what it means or what we can do with it. But that's just how it seems to be."

"Well, it is definitely helpful in this healing we are doing. I hope that we can do more of this, because I get more out of our phone calls than any class, that's for sure. Do you think you could teach me to bring healing to you over the phone too? I would really like to practice my healing skills, see if I can feel it from the other end, and also be able to give it back to you. This keeps a balance between us."

"I would like that too. Like I said, I don't have anyone who can do healing work for me, so I would be grateful for that. Let's plan on that for next time."

"Awesome! This will be fun!"

They said goodbye and made arrangements for their next phone call. Lily sat and contemplated all that had happened. She decided to write it all down in her journal so she wouldn't forget any details. The experience was already indelibly etched on her memory and her heart. How does one categorize and process something that is so unbelievable and profound? Her mind didn't have any boxes to put this in. Maybe it was time to make some new boxes, or let it exist outside the box. Her mind still wanted to know what it all meant. What was this connection really about? As she lay there deep in thought, she dozed off.

Her healing, training and messages continued as she slept. One angel worked with her on healing skills, another was sitting with her talking like an old friend, and the last she remembered was a group of angels gathered around her as she lay flat, their hands on her for healing. She could see them removing tons of old garbage from her body. A broken bicycle wheel, a sword, a long bone from an animal, an old cassette player ... Where did all this junk come from? At least they were removing it, so she would certainly feel better after it was all cleared away.

As soon as she woke, she journaled about the "dreams" she had. They were different from her usual dreams. They seemed to have really happened, and not just because they seemed so vivid, it was more of a knowing. She felt energized and light. *Could this be real? Could the angels really have helped me while I slept?* In her mind and heart, she felt a resounding, "YES!"

Chapter 16

After having a long-distance healing session with Frank, I definitely feel a powerful energy between us. It is as if we are both amped up to the highest degree whenever we are together, even if it's over the phone. It seems we bring out each other's best selves, and in the biggest and brightest way possible. It really is an amazing gift! I'm not going to ask again what this means or why. I am just saying "Thank you," savoring the gift and taking in all the blessings that come with it. My soul feels happy, joyful and at peace with all of this. I will take that as a good sign.

~Lily's journal

Needing someone to help her sort out all the things that were whirling around in her head, Lily invited Maria to come over to chat. They had spoken on the phone a couple times since they met, but this was the first time they got together.

"I'm so happy to see you again!" Lily greeted her with a

big hug as Maria glided up the sidewalk. She brought some fresh baked shortbread cookies with her. "Mmm, these look delicious! Would it be alright with you if we sat out here on these lawn chairs? I just hate being inside on such a beautiful evening."

"That would be lovely."

"I'll just grab the lemonade and be right back." Lily disappeared into the house and returned with a tray carrying a pitcher and two glasses. She placed them on the patio table in the back yard. It was shady, and a nice cool breeze was flowing through the yard, a comfortable place to sit and chat on a hot summer evening.

"I'm so glad you called me. I've thought of you often and wondered how you were doing. What did you think of the healing workshop you took?" Maria asked as she poured herself a tall glass of lemonade.

"I loved it! I don't know what it is about energy healing that seems to spark something deep within me. I'm not sure yet what that will mean for me in my life, but I definitely want to learn more and practice more." Lily poured her own glass. "We didn't get to talk much that first day. Do you use energy healing much in your massage work?"

"I do use it some, but I would like to do more of it. I know that I could make greater profound changes with the energy work than I can with massage, and without the wear and tear on my body. It's a matter of convincing my clients of it. They are used to physical touch everywhere, digging into the areas that are sore. It is a whole different mindset, realizing that pain and tightness can be alleviated from within using energy. The people that have been open to trying it are amazed. Feeling is believing, I guess. Others just don't want to give up the massages that they are used to, don't want change. That doesn't keep me from adding some energy healing to the massage. They just think I have magic hands!" Maria laughed as she reclined back in the chair.

"And maybe you do have magic hands! Who's to say you don't. I was with a patient recently who was in terrible pain, had been in a car accident and sustained multiple fractures and injuries. He had all the prescribed pain medication, but his pain was still intractable, and his blood pressure was climbing because of it. There was nothing I could do but try to make him comfortable while waiting for his doctor. I decided to put my hands on his chest and told him to close his eyes and take slow breaths. I brought in some healing energy for him just for a couple minutes, to allow the warm healing light to flow through his body. It didn't take long for his blood pressure to stabilize and his pain to decrease enough for him to fall asleep. It was amazing! The frustrating part is I couldn't tell anybody about it. I know what you mean about the different mindset. Working as a nurse in a hospital, I'm noticing more and more that I don't agree with traditional ways anymore. So many of the patients could really benefit from energy healing and other alternative methods, but there is no way I can openly do that there, and can't even suggest it. I have a feeling that once I learn more and feel more confident in my skills, I'll be leaving nursing. That's kind of a scary idea. I have always loved what I do. Suddenly it doesn't seem to fit me anymore, like I'm outgrowing it. It's strange how quickly and unexpectedly things can change, isn't it?"

"I think that is especially true when you are on a spiritual path. Once you start making decisions in alignment with your soul, things happen super fast!"

"Like a runaway train, I'd say!" Lily laughed and reached for a cookie.

"So what else is happening that is hijacking your life as you knew it?" Maria asked as she sipped her drink.

"Oh, where do I start? My life in a nutshell ... I've been dating Derrick for over a year. He's anxious to get married. I love him, but there's something that holds me back. I keep him at a distance, and I'm afraid to commit. I do have old trust issues that I've been working on, but I'm not sure that's it." She took a sip of her lemonade and a deep breath before continuing. "Anyway, at the workshop I met a man that I really connected with. His name is Frank. I felt like I'd known him forever. We really click, have so many similar interests, and also similar experiences even though we come from completely different backgrounds. He lives a couple hours away, so I haven't seen him since, but we talk on the phone once a week, for usually a couple hours at a time. I've never met anyone that I could talk with so easily. This is the first time I've ever met someone who seems to really get me. When he looks at me or even listens to me talk, I can tell he truly sees me and is deeply listening to every word I say. We are just friends, but it is confusing to me, this deep connection we have. I've been trying to figure it out ever since we met. What do you think this means?" Lily exhaled after rattling all that off at one time. "I'm starting to think I should have made margaritas instead of lemonade!"

"No kidding! I don't know what it means, but I want to meet him!" Maria joked. "Especially if you are just friends. I'm kidding." Maria laughed and then sat looking thoughtfully at her glass, digesting all that Lily had said. "Seriously, though, I believe that making a deep connection like this is important, even if it is just as a passing acquaintance. No doubt you've been together before. Sorting out the past life emotions from the present ones can be tricky. A strong bond like this can make life seem a little distorted at times."

"What do you mean, distorted?"

"The past life experiences and emotional baggage that goes with it can bring up emotions from the past. This sometimes makes it seem like this is what your heart wants, when your heart is just remembering how it was in another lifetime."

"So how can I sort that out?"

"Connect to your soul, ask it to clear away the baggage and emotion from the past, and see clearly what is true in the present. You can do this in meditation or journaling, or you can set this as your intention in a healing session as well. It won't be easy, it seems like you two are already emotionally entangled."

"I'll try that. Yes, I do feel like a tangled-up mess," Lily admitted, as she grabbed another cookie. "These are the best cookies! I hope you don't mind that I'm pigging out on them. I don't usually eat sweets like this, but I can't help myself tonight."

"Knock yourself out. I brought them here so that I wouldn't eat the entire batch myself," Maria confessed, as she also reached for another one.

"My plan is to continue to do my own inner work ... healing, meditation, journaling, yoga ... all the things that help me to connect with my soul, with the intention to clear away the old memories holding me back. Hopefully as I do that all these problems will work themselves out and all will become clear to me."

"That sounds like a great plan. Does Derrick know about Frank?" Maria asked.

"No, I was never sure how to broach that subject. A part of me feels guilty about that, although we are just friends. I'm not sure how Derrick would feel about me being such good friends with another man."

"Don't you think you'll have to tell him before you marry him?"

"Yes, definitely. If Frank and I are still friends when that time comes, if that time comes, I would want Derrick to understand and accept our friendship."

"Do you think he would? Most men would be threatened by their wife having a close friendship with another man."

"He doesn't seem to be the jealous type, but this would be pushing the envelope."

"Next time we talk, we'll have to dissect your relationship with Derrick, and figure out what's going on there. Take that as a warning," Maria teased her.

"OK, I've been warned. Thanks for saving it for next time. I really don't think I can go there right now."

"Don't put off our getting together just to avoid it, though."

"I won't. How about next week, is that soon enough for you?" They planned out their next meeting and then continued to chat, changing the focus to Maria's love life for another hour.

After Maria left, Lily sat out in the moonlight and

thought about all that was said. Was she really confused about old past-life baggage, or were these present-day feelings? Sure felt like a big old tangled mess to her. The question was how to untangle it without getting tied up in it. One could find themselves tied up by their feet upside down, if they are not careful. She chuckled at her own analogy, imagining herself hanging by her feet in the jungle, suspended by vines, as snakes and other frightening creatures lined the ground beneath her. (Shudder) *Alright, so I need to sort through the vines without getting caught up in the knots. Don't get ensnared. That's easy for you to say,* she told herself, gathering the dishes to go inside for the night. Maybe she could ask her angels to help her untangle while she slept ... now that was a good idea!

Chapter 17

"Focus on what is truly important and let the rest go."

This is what popped into my head as I sat to meditate and clear my mind. It makes sense: focus on what's important and let the rest go. The problem is that all of the things spinning around in my head seem important to me. How do I know what is not important? If it didn't seem important, I wouldn't be obsessing over it, now, would I. Maybe "truly" is the operative word here. What is TRULY important? Soul, please show me what is TRULY important.

As I close my eyes and take a breath, I hear, "You know."

~Lily's journal

Derrick made an unprecedented visit to Lily at the hospital in the middle of her shift. The charge nurse at the nursing station pointed him to the group of rooms where she worked, but wasn't sure exactly where she was or when she would be free. He agreed to just wait until she came out into the hallway. He was in no hurry, but he kept shifting his position, unable to stand still.

Lily came out of a nearby room and almost ran into him, then stopped dead in her tracks, shocked to see him. "What are you doing here? What's wrong?" She assumed he was in the hospital for some health reason.

"Nothing's wrong. I hope it's okay that I came by. I just had the inspiration to stop by and ask you to dinner?" His excitement and anticipation was contagious, and he could barely hold it in.

"Yes, absolutely! I'd love to have dinner with you!" She gave him a quick kiss. "What time?"

"Just come when you're done with work. I can't wait!"

"I need to get back to work. I'll see you again as soon I'm done here. Thanks for coming by, that's such a nice surprise!" Derrick left, and Lily continued with her work day. She thought about this spontaneous invitation. It was weird that he would come by at work, in the middle of the day, and not just call or send her a text. And he seemed very excited about a simple dinner date. Something was up ...

On her way out, something in the gift shop window caught her eye, a wooden plaque, rustic in appearance, with the words, "Cabin, Sweet, Cabin," painted on it. She couldn't resist buying it for Derrick. He hadn't said anything further about the cabin, but she needed to get it anyway to show her support if he did buy it. The clerk even gift-wrapped it for her so she wouldn't have to stop at home first.

As she drove into Derrick's driveway, he was loading a bag into his car. "Are you going somewhere? I thought we were just having dinner."

He came up and gave her a kiss and hug. "We are having dinner, just not here."

"I came straight from work. Do I need to go home and change clothes? I'm not dressed for a restaurant."

Derrick laughed softly. "No, you don't need to change. It won't be anything fancy. Just get in, I'm hungry."

She sneaked her gift bag into the back seat and climbed in beside him. "So where are we going?"

"I called the owners of the cabin, to ask them a few more questions. She said I should just go back to the cabin to see for myself. So, I thought since you were coming over for dinner, I would bring you with me. We can have dinner there and look around, take measurements, find the answers to my questions. Is that alright with you?"

"Of course, that's a great idea! It will be fun to see it again. I'm sure we will see things differently, or at least from a different perspective now that you are considering buying it."

"Well, I hope it doesn't look too different. I guess that's why I wanted to have another look, because I wasn't really focused on it the first time. I might have only been seeing the good that weekend, now I want to see everything, so I know what I'm getting and what would be a fair price."

"I think that's a smart way to do it. Hopefully we can see what we need to before it gets dark."

"I brought some burritos. We can either eat them in the car on the way or wait until we get there."

"Since it is an hour and a half drive, I vote to eat on the way. I don't know if I could wait that long. How about you?"

"I agree, they smell too good to wait."

Lily got Derrick's food ready while he drove. It was all wrapped up so he could eat with one hand and drive with the other. She ate hers as well, and they talked casually and listened to music along the drive.

Pulling into the driveway of the cabin, it did appear to be different. They didn't just see it as a cheap place to stay for a weekend, but instead one that could be theirs. Even the maintenance that needed to be done was something they could do together to make this place great. They saw both the fix-it projects, and the potential. Derrick brought a notebook to keep track of what needed to be done. He would later calculate how much it would cost him to make these improvements to help him to negotiate a fair price. They also measured all of the rooms, and considered everything that was in each room. They made a list of the things that they would like to stay, and what could go. It would be nice to not have to find all new furnishings, especially since money would be tight from the purchase price.

Once they completed their inventory of furnishings and fix-it projects, they watched the sunset from the swing. Derrick put his arm around her and pulled her close. Lily snuggled in and asked, "So what do you think? After looking at everything with a magnifying glass, has your opinion changed? Is it still what you want?"

"Yes, and I'm glad we came tonight. It really helped me to have a clear picture of what I'm bidding on, what needs to be fixed, what it will cost to get it into shape. I can see doing some projects just to get it comfortable and looking nice, but eventually, I would like to add on to it, make it bigger and more open. Adding a master suite and a screen porch would also be nice. I would like to make one of those outdoor dining areas with a fireplace oven. There are so many possibilities for what we could do here. And I'm so glad that you are here to help with all of that. I love that we are figuring it out together. It feels really good! What do you think?"

"I agree, I hadn't looked as closely at this last time. And hadn't paid much attention to what was in the cabin then. It's going to take quite a bit of work to get it in shape, but at least it's not a long drive for us." She looked out over the lake as a loon flew by, calling out as it went. "And there's no better place than right here to watch the sunset."

"You're right about that. I have a feeling this is going to be a very good investment."

She pulled the gift bag out she had hidden behind the tree while he was taking measurements inside. "Here, I brought you a little gift. It may be a little premature, but when I saw it I couldn't resist. And now that we are here, it seems perfect."

He opened the bag and pulled out the wall hanging. He chuckled, saying, "This is great! I think I know exactly where we will hang it. Thank you. This really means a lot to me." He leaned over and kissed her. They sat watching the sunset for a while before making the trip back home.

The evening went well. They hadn't fought about anything. It really did seem right for Derrick to buy this cabin. She loved the serendipity of how it all came together, finding this place just when they needed a place for a weekend, and the owners deciding to sell just when Derrick decided he wanted it. Everything seemed to be falling into place perfectly. *The question is ... is it falling into place for me and Derrick, or is this just for Derrick? Is this a sign that*

I should pay attention to? It seems so, but what is it trying to tell me? I wish the signs could be a little more direct and straight-forward, leaving no room for interpretation. Is that too much to ask?

Chapter 18

Today is my phone session with Frank. My turn to try out my long-distance sensors. I'm a little nervous about this. What if I can't do it? I don't want him to know I'm no good at this. I don't want him to see me fail. Oh, these issues again. Soul, please help me to set aside my fears. Help me to know and sense the gifts that I can use for Frank. Any advice on how I can do this?

Connection, intuition, love, and healing. Make your connections ... to your soul, angels, Frank's soul ... and trust! Believe in yourself! You can do it!

~Lily's journal

On Friday, Frank called Lily at their scheduled time. They talked for a while about all that had happened during the week since they last talked. Frank told about some issues he was having with his family. "My ex has always been a drama queen, and difficult to deal with, always doing whatever she can to get her own way. Now my kids are at the ages where they know just the right buttons to push. They have grown up watching their mom push my buttons and now know them all too well. They are generally good kids, and I'm proud of that, but sometimes ... ugh!"

"I can't imagine how difficult that must be. I can feel your frustration as you talk about this. But I also feel how much you love your kids. You are proud of them, but also afraid of them learning their parents' behaviors and making the same mistakes."

"That's exactly right, although I hadn't really put that together. They are at the ages when my ex and I got together. You know when you are seventeen and in love, you think you know everything, and won't listen to anyone. You feel like nobody can possibly understand what you are going through. Now I can see that my mom tried to warn me, but I wouldn't listen. My kids have been my greatest gift, I wouldn't trade them for the world, but I hope they choose an easier path than I did."

"That's the thing, isn't it? They will choose their path. I bet that's the hardest thing for a parent, letting them choose, even if you see what that path will bring for them."

"Yes, you just hope that you taught them well, and gave them a good enough foundation to make the right choices. I guess that's all I can really do. And be there when they need me."

"I'm sure they do know you are there for them. You've always been there for them. Even if they butt heads with you, deep down they know you love them."

"You're right. I truly believe they know that. It's one of the things that has always been most important to me, that they know how much I care about them and that I am always there for them, no matter what."

It was apparent how much love Frank held for his kids, and it was impressive. Did all parents feel this way? Her family was not so open with affection. She always knew she was loved, but it was never outwardly expressed.

"So, are you still interested in me trying out some long-distance healing on you?"

"Absolutely! I think this all has come up for me for that purpose, I'm ready for healing today. I'm so glad you are willing to try it. I'll go over the basics, but it really is not much different than what we did in person. The main difference is that you are connecting with my energy through your mind instead of your hands. You can still hold your hands as if you are touching me, if that helps you visualize or feel the energy, but it is really your individual preference. Personally, I like to use my hands to move the energy just like I do in person." Frank gave Lily a few more detailed instructions on what to imagine, how to call in the energy, how to connect with his energy, and set the intention for the session. He revealed that he always said a prayer before starting each healing, either out loud or to himself, to create a safe sacred healing space, to make the divine connections, and to set the intention for the healing.

Lily followed his instructions, she took a deep breath, she said a prayer for herself and for the session, calling in angels to assist her with the healing. She felt the connection immediately and knew they were there to help. She held her hands up, like they were on his invisible shoulders, and the energy began to flow from the divine through her, out through her hands and into Frank. She imagined connecting her energy with Frank. She felt his energy very strongly. His agitation, frustration and fear was almost overwhelming to her. She felt his emotions in her body as if they were her own. The emotions intensified, the anger and frustration in her chest was burning hot, with heavy pressure, and felt like it might explode. Just when she thought she might not be able to stand it any longer, it shifted. The agitation, anger and frustration dissipated. There was still fear and also sadness. The outer layer had cleared, and now she was on a deeper level.

Frank described what he was feeling, validating what Lily sensed. He also revealed memories and images that came to him as he tuned in to these feelings. It brought him back to when he was a child, five years old. It was as if he was that little boy again, even his voice sounded different as he talked about what was happening. "I'm scared. Don't leave me. I don't want to be alone."

His mom worked a second job, stocking shelves at a grocery store. She started at 10pm. She didn't leave until after Frank was asleep, and usually got home about 5am, before he woke up. She was unaware that he woke up when she shut the door to leave. He lay there crying and trembling in his bed. He was hyper-aware of every noise in the house, and flicker of light coming in the window. In the dark of his bedroom, he felt alone and abandoned and afraid.

"What does that little boy Frank need right now to feel safe? Imagine him receiving whatever that is," Lily offered softly and compassionately.

"He wants to be held. He wants his mom to come home and hold him as he sleeps. He would feel safe then."

"Imagine his mom being there with him, aware of how he is feeling. Feel how it would feel for him to be held by his mom, safe and loved. And let him feel that he is being taken care of. He can relax and let go. He is safe, and he is loved." Frank let out a loud sigh and the muscles in his chest and arms muscles visibly relaxed. "Is there anything his mom wants to say to him now to express her understanding of how scared he was to be alone?"

"She feels so bad. She's crying. She thought she was doing the right thing. She says she's sorry for hurting him, that she loves him. He hugs her and says that it's ok, he forgives her." Frank sniffles into the phone.

"Feel divine light surrounding both of them. Let the light clear away any of the fear, sadness and pain. Feel the warmth of love and peace flowing in to heal them both. Take some time to let that light flow through every cell of your body, through you and around you." Lily could feel a gentle vibration and warmth moving through her own body; she was buzzing all over, but also felt extremely calm and relaxed.

Lily slipped into a deeper consciousness as well. She felt weightless and like she was somewhere else entirely. There was light everywhere. It felt comfortable and inviting. She let herself be immersed in it. Immersed in love. Love was everywhere, all around her. There were other beings there as well, all showering her with love. It was difficult to tell what they looked like because they were light of varying hues. How is it possible to feel so much love? Then she noticed Frank was there too. They were both surrounded by this giant ball of glowing love. As they turned toward each other they were united and connected in this amazing love energy. Streams of light connected their hearts and their energy fields. Then they seemed to merge together into one being. She could not see or feel any difference between them, they had become one being. It was blissfully perfect, with no worries, no pains, just love and light. They stayed in that oneness for quite a while (outside of time and space), then it all faded away and they were back in the present.

Frank was silent for quite a while, then took a deep breath and sighed. "Wow! That was deep stuff! I don't even remember that far back, I didn't remember my mom leaving me alone, but it felt so real. I definitely believe it happened. I feel so much lighter now. It is amazing how something like that can weigh on you so many years later."

Lily took a moment to be fully present. "Does it feel like those worries and fears really cleared from you?" Lily asked hesitantly. She was having difficulty remembering anything from before the love fest.

"Yes, that definitely made a big difference. That was a big moment with my mom. We haven't had a very good relationship. Besides the money issues of being a single parent, she also had some boyfriends that were abusive to me. She never had what I would consider a good healthy relationship. I know I still have a lot to heal with her. I have made a conscious effort to do things differently with my kids than the way I was raised. Healing this feeling of abandonment today will make a big difference. I have already been working on healing the anger, resentment and trauma from the abuse. One step at a time."

"I'm glad it was helpful. Any feedback on my part in the session?"

"You were amazing! Your questions were right on, and you gave me just the right cues to keep me going and let me have time in silence to allow it to complete. Excellent job! I can't believe that was your first time! You're a natural at this!"

"It was interesting how the words just seemed to come to me at the right moment. And they were not even my words."

"That's the divine flowing through you. Call it angels, or God, or light beings, but they were helping you the entire time. It's great that you are able to open to them like that."

"I've been working on that a lot in meditation and in my journaling. Maybe that is helping in the healing area too."

"I'm sure that makes a difference. But you need to be aware that you have a gift here. I'm not just saying that to make you feel good. That was a truly powerful session!"

"Thanks, I appreciate that. And I'm grateful for your teaching me and showing me how it is done." Lily took a breath, gathering the courage to learn more. "Can I ask you something?"

"Of course."

"What did you experience after the healing with your mom, when the light came into your body, up until the end of the session? What was that like for you?"

He chuckled. "Yeah, that was intense. I've never experienced anything like it before. I expected the light to move through me like it usually does, but this was different. I'm not quite sure what to think of it just yet. It was in some other dimension, surrounded by loving beings. The most loving place I've ever felt or imagined. I didn't ask who they were or what they wanted, I was just so enthralled with the feeling of love. I could have stayed there forever! They probably knew I had no desire to return, because all of a sudden I was back in my body."

"I'm not sure if I lost my grounding or how it happened,

but I was pulled into that part of the session. I really don't know what happened, but I was there with you. We were both having our separate experiences and then we were together for a while. And then we were back. I wish I understood what happened and what it means."

"I don't have any answers either. This is new territory for me as well. Maybe we just need to accept it as a gift and be grateful for the experience and what it brought us, without trying to figure it out. It was unbelievable!"

"That's true. I would like to journal about it, but I know I won't be able to do it justice, there just aren't words that could adequately fit the feelings or the experience."

"I know I'm going to sit with this for a while and let it sink in, then meditate, or maybe I'll write or paint to capture it as accurately as I can. I don't want it to slip away."

"I'll let you go then. Thank you so much for guiding me on this and for trusting me to practice on you."

"And thank you for leading this amazing session. Have a great week! Text me your schedule and we'll figure out a time for our next call."

"Okey dokey, you have a wonderful week too!" They hung up the phone and Lily lay back on the couch and closed her eyes. She recalled the feeling of love from the session. And tried to bask in it for a little while longer.

Her thoughts kept going to Frank and the intense love she felt with him at the end of the session. What was that about? What did it mean that they were in this "Love Land" together? They were surrounded by love, but there was also love between them, she was sure of it. And then they had merged into one. She accepted that it was a great gift they had been given, but that didn't mean she could just write it off without asking questions. This wasn't just a random dream. They were both brought into this loving space by the light beings who were helping with the healing. It had to have some meaning or message for them, and she didn't want to miss it. *What are you trying to tell us? What does this mean?*

Chapter 19

I can't stop thinking about the intense love I felt in that session with Frank. That is what I've always dreamed of having. Someone I connected with on all levels. A love that transcends all time and space. That sounds like a made-for-TV movie, but now that I have experienced it with Frank, I can't think of anything else. He has to feel the same way, since we both experienced it. Right? Soul, can you give me some hints here?

Patience, there's more to unfold.

~Lily's journal

Lily went to work each day, doing everything that she was supposed to do, but her mind was always somewhere else. It was a miracle that she managed to give all of her patients the right medications and treatments at the right times. Angels must have been helping with that, because she definitely wasn't present with anything that she was doing. Her mind was consumed by thoughts of Frank.

At lunch, her friend Nicki called her out on it. "What is

the matter with you? I've never seen you so spacey. It's like you are somewhere else. Wherever it is, I hope it's someplace nice!" She teased.

Lily sighed. "I've told you about the man I met at the healing workshop, right?"

"I think so, yes, what about him?"

She paused, trying to decide if she should disclose this to Nicki or not. But since she'd started, she needed to follow through. "I think I might be in love with him." She blurted it out quickly, as if to decrease the comprehension of what she was saying.

"What? How can you be in love with him? Have you seen him since?"

"No, I haven't seen him, but we talk on the phone a lot."

"What about Derrick?" Nicki asked.

"I don't know. I'm so confused. I still love Derrick, but this is different."

"Does this guy know how you feel? Does he feel the same way about you?"

Looking down at her hands, Lily confessed, "I haven't told him. I don't know if he feels the same way. I have a feeling he does, but I'm not sure. I'm going to have to talk to him about it. But I'm such a chicken. What if he doesn't love me? Then what happens to our friendship? And what if he does? I feel like I'm going insane."

"You know I'm no expert in this kind of thing, but it seems to me like you are trying to figure out something with your head that needs to be done with the heart. And maybe you just need to wait to see how things go the next time you talk to Frank, and if he says anything or gives you any clues about how he feels."

"That's good advice. I like that idea. I'll try to be cool on my end and see if he lets anything slip. And in the meantime, I need to find a way to put it out of my mind so that I can function like a normal human being again. Any ideas about that?"

"Well, you could start by enjoying one of those amazing desserts. That should pull you back into the present."

"I like how you think. You need to have one too. If I'm going down, I'm taking you with me." They laughed and picked out their desserts, savoring every bite before going back to work.

After her shift ended, Lily sat in her car. Where should she go? Thankfully she didn't have any plans for this evening. She needed to do something to clear her head and become more connected with herself. Meditation, walks outside, yoga ... all of that would be good. She'd start with a walk outside, find a place to sit and meditate along the way. Then come home to have something to eat, then attend a yoga class. Pleased that she now had a plan, she drove home to change clothes and get started on her evening of self-care.

She chose to go to a park that she knew well. It was near her house and had walking paths, but also had a lake and streams, woods, rocks and benches to sit on. Hopefully there wouldn't be too many people out tonight. She needed solitude.

She started off briskly walking on the path. Letting her thoughts come and go, she worked her way through some of them. She realized that some of this was drama she had created in her own mind. She laughed to herself. *"I am actually driving myself crazy. "* Her emphasis was on herself. *"This is all of my own making. It can be simple, or it can be complicated. How do I want it to be?"* Her thoughts continued as she walked. *"I do want it to be simple. How can it be simple? Is that possible?"*

A voice in her head answered, *"Of course. Anything is possible."*

"Okay, I'll go with that. I want it to be simple. Help me to make it simple."

She found a bench at the side of a stream. The bench faced the water. No one else was around. *"Please identify yourself. I need to know who is helping me now."* She closed her eyes and the image of an angel in lovely pink light was in front of her. *"Are you my guardian angel?"* She knew as she asked the question that it was true, she also felt the yes coming from her angel. *"Thank you for being here. I could really use your help right now."* A feather floated in on the breeze and landed on the bench next to her.

She sat gazing into the water, losing herself in the gentle sounds of water, birds, and leaves in the breeze. Watching the water easily move around obstacles, flowing around rocks, sticks, and earth, she felt her worries wash away. She slipped into a deep space of surrender and acceptance. She saw an image of herself floating down a river, peacefully and easily. *"Go with the flow."*

"What about making decisions? How does that fit into the go with the flow idea?"

"When you go with the flow your decisions will be made with ease as you are not forcing yourself to go against the flow of the river, or the flow of your soul," her angel replied.

"Isn't it bad to just take the easy way?"

"I don't mean choosing the easiest option. The decision will be easier to make because it is in alignment with your truth and will come to you easier. Connecting to your truth is going with the flow of your soul. The decisions made from that space just seem right and easy, even if the actions that go with them may be difficult."

"So, you're saying if I continue to connect with my soul and my truth, I will know what to do without so much stress?"

"Exactly."

Lily sat with this concept for a while, as the water continued to flow through the stream and the breeze continued to flow through the trees. Wouldn't that make it very simple if all I had to do was focus on connecting with my soul and my truth and let everything else fall into place, acting only on what feels right for me?

She took a deep breath and let out the weight of her stress with her exhale. Her shoulders relaxed, and she sank more deeply into the bench. The sun slipped past the trees as it moved lower in the sky, and now warmed her shoulders with its soft rays.

"Thank you for your help. I like this new approach. Please help me to be able to break my old habits and try this new way of thinking and being."

Chapter 20

Connect with my soul and my truth, go with the flow and let everything fall into place, acting on what feels right. Seems so simple, but not so much when you are trying to live it.

Stop trying so hard.

If I stop trying won't I just go back to my old habits?

It's more about being and allowing than trying. One step at a time.

How do I do that?

Believe and trust in yourself.

I'm working on that, which is actually trying to break an old habit. As you said, one step at a time.

~Lily's journal

L ily had Saturday off. Her work schedule had been kind of funky lately, and she'd worked the past 10 days straight. She'd picked up a shift for someone who had sprained her ankle, so that made her week extra-long. She was grateful for the sunny day, and a chance to be outside. Derrick invited her over to help with some landscaping, and then dinner later.

Lily was looking forward to working outside, but when she pulled into Derrick's driveway, her chest tightened as a wave of anxiety hit her. How am I going to spend the day with Derrick when I am so confused about my feelings? She sat in the car for a couple minutes, trying to calm herself. She took some deep breaths, forcing her heart to slow down a little.

Her new mantra popped into her head, "Connect; Go with the flow; Allow it to fall into place; Act on what feels right." She connected with her soul, feeling the light within her core. Taking another deep breath, she sighed. "Ok, I can do this. I will enjoy this day and all of the good that it brings me."

She got out of the car and entered the house. Derrick was in the kitchen drinking coffee. "Hey, good morning, beautiful! I thought I heard you drive up, but then when you didn't come in I thought maybe it was the neighbors." He came over and gave her a quick kiss.

"I was just getting my things together. Looks like we have perfect weather to be outside," she answered defensively. It was weird to feel so awkward about him kissing her. She felt herself putting up an invisible force-field. She was really needing her space today, but she didn't know how to ask for that without hurting his feelings or making an issue of it.

"Yes, I'm excited to get this project going. It's going to be a lot of work to get the grass out of that area, but at least it is under a tree, so we'll have some shade." He wanted to create an area under the tree for a bench, some plants and eventually a pond. But right now it was still a grassy, weedy part of the lawn. The grass didn't grow well there, but there was still a lot to clear out.

Derrick carved out the area that would be the new garden space and started the edging it to frame it. Lily focused on digging up the grass and weeds. It felt good to work in the dirt and focus on such a simple task. It became meditative after a while. Her mind began to clear, and she took the opportunity to connect more fully to her soul and to the earth she was digging in. It was hard work and her back was stiff, her muscles ached, but it was exactly what she needed today.

They took a break for lunch. Lily was still in a contemplative space, enjoying the sunshine as they ate on the patio. Derrick looked at her, his brow furrowed with concern. "You are so quiet today. Is everything ok?"

"I seem to be introspective today, even before I got here. Could be from working so many days in a row. Being outside pulling these weeds feels therapeutic for me. I'm sorry I'm not better company."

"Well, let me know if there is anything I can do to help. If you would rather rest, we can do more later."

"Thanks, I appreciate that. But it feels good for me to work in the dirt. This is exactly what I need today."

They continued gardening a couple more hours, until the sun moved, and their area was now in the sun and blistering hot. Derrick stood up and wiped sweat from his forehead.

"How about some cold drinks and shade?"

"Sounds wonderful!" Lily slowly got up and stretched her back and neck. She plopped down in one of the cushy chairs on the deck. "Where's a massage therapist when you need one?"

Derrick brought her a glass of ice water. He then stood behind her and started to massage her shoulders. She felt herself flinch and tighten at first, then reminded herself that it was ok to go with the flow. The massage did feel good, and she let her muscles relax. It's not as if she didn't trust Derrick, she just didn't trust herself at the moment. The guilt she felt for all of her thoughts and confusion about Frank was gnawing away at her.

"Thank you, I didn't realize I was so tense."

"That's a start, I can do more later. It's the least I can do for all your hard work here. Are you sure there is nothing bothering you? You just don't seem yourself today."

"I'm sorry, I guess I'm a little stressed. I've been feeling more and more that I don't really want to continue in nursing anymore. I know that I need to keep my job to pay the bills, and to enable me to eventually do what I'm passionate about."

"And what is it that you're passionate about?"

"I'm sure you will think this is crazy, but I really love energy healing. It lights me up like nothing else I've done. I know that it will take some time to complete more classes and gain the experience and confidence I need, but eventually I would like to do that as my profession and have my own business."

"Like I've said before, I don't understand that. Maybe my brain just doesn't work that way. Give me numbers, they either add up or they don't, which makes sense to me. I can see that you would get tired of working the crazy schedule you have at the hospital. Maybe they could transfer you to another department where you would have regular hours, like at a clinic. Then you wouldn't lose your seniority and those great benefits. After we're married I can support us both, and you can stay home with the kids if you want to. Would that make you happy?"

Lily was a little taken aback by how he really didn't understand what she was trying to say, or how she was feeling. *Did he even hear what I said?* She decided it best to let it be for right now, not having the energy for an argument right now, almost shaking her head in disbelief. Even though she was going to let the argument go, everything he said would stay with her.

"Well, I'm not really sure what I want right now. I need more time to figure it out, I guess."

"Just let me know how I can help. I'm here for you, you know." Derrick patted her hand on the table.

"Thanks, I appreciate that." Lily smiled back at him pensively, still feeling uneasy about what he said. "So, Boss, are we going to do more work in the garden today? Or are we done for now?"

"I think it's too hot out there now. We'll have to come back to it another day."

"Sounds good to me! I'm going to shower and change, then I'll meet you back here." Lily went inside to grab her backpack with a change of clothes.

"How would you like a pina colada when you get out?"

"Mmm! That would be heavenly! I won't take long." Lily

hustled off into the guest bathroom to take her shower.

"Take your time. It will be ready when you are."

As promised, her frosty drink was waiting for her. A beer sat out for him, he obviously had made the pina colada just for her. Very thoughtful of him.

Derrick had evidently gone to clean himself up, too. She took her drink out to a reclining chair on the deck, now in full shade. It felt so good to sit there in the cool breeze, out of the sun, with a tropical drink in her hand. She closed her eyes and sank back into the chair. All of her worries melted away. She was happy and content. What was I so stressed about all day? I'm not going to let my worries ruin this beautiful afternoon. Right now, all that matters is relaxing in this chair, outside on this gorgeous day, sipping a yummy drink. My problems can wait for another time.

Chapter 21

When I connect with my soul and I think of Derrick, I feel comfortable and safe, as if sitting in front of a warm fireplace. When I think of Frank, I feel myself expand and radiate light all around me. I am powerful, brilliant, and full of love. These are all good feelings, but what does that mean? Which one is better? Soul, please help me to know what is right for me.

Trust yourself, the answers are within you.

~Lily's Journal

T he dream came out of nowhere, though isn't that the way of all dreams. Lily and Frank were walking along the beach, holding hands and enjoying the sun, ocean waves, cool breeze, the hot sand under their bare feet. Lily spread her arms out and stood on the edge of the water. The sun warmed her face, while the misty ocean breeze cooled her. She twirled around, soaking it all in, almost dancing on the beach. "I can't believe how beautiful it is here. I feel so alive and so blessed!"

Frank came to stand in front of her, inches away from her face. He placed his hands on hers, palm to palm, arms still outstretched. Their hands were the only point of contact. They began to slowly turn and move together, a beautiful dance of unity and oneness. Arms moving in sync, with bodies slowly twisting and turning in the breeze. After a while their movements slowed to where they were standing still, palms still touching. As they looked deeply into each other's eyes, the rest of the world ceased to exist. They slipped into some other place of deep connection. Their souls were reunited in a blissful state of oneness.

Time and space seemed to disappear. They may have been there for hours or it may have only been seconds. Still only aware of each other, their lips came together. Electric energy surged through them both. They were surrounded by a light of infinite colors. Floating and spinning through the universe, but not in the darkness of space, they were enveloped in this psychedelic light. Pure love flowed through them as they connected on all levels. They were one and joined by the deepest love. This love filled them both and radiated all around them.

Eventually their awareness came back to the beach where they stood, hands and lips touching. The feelings of love still flowing through them, they began to kiss, and their arms wrapped to hold each other tightly in a passionate embrace. The intense energies of what had just taken place fueled the fires of their physical desire and passion.

Lily woke feeling hot and sweaty, wrapped up in her sheets. She lay there replaying the scenes of the dream and savoring the feelings of love and passion. It was an amazing dream, very vivid, and the energy of it extremely potent. Wow! She tried to catch her breath. How could a dream leave her breathless?

The longer she lay there, the more her mind tried to continue the scene in the dream to see what would happen next. It was the best dream she had ever experienced, and she would have loved to stay there all day. She did get out of bed eventually, needing to get ready for work.

Of course, then her thoughts immediately began analyzing the dream. Was this a demonstration of what her soul really wanted? Was this just her mind taking her connection to Frank and her desire for true love to new levels, creating a fantasy for her? Was there a deeper message here? Maybe it had nothing to do with Frank.

She got out her journal to quickly write down as many details about the dream as possible, even though she knew it was the sort of dream she would remember forever and was burned on her brain. After she finished her writing and was ready to leave for work, she knew she was going to need some help figuring this one out. Who should she call? Maria. They had already planned to go for a walk after work tonight. This was perfect!

After work, Lily met Maria at a park where they could walk the trails and talk. They greeted each other with hugs and began their walk. "I've never been to this park. It's lovely, and not as busy as the ones near my apartment," Lily commented.

"This is my favorite place to hike and enjoy nature. And you're right, it's like a hidden treasure in the city. I hope it stays that way. I love that it is so peaceful and secluded, away from people, even though we are still technically in the city." Maria gazed over her treasured paradise, this park, as her appreciation for it filled her.

"How is everything going for you?" Lily asked.

"It is going well. I think I'm going to have to find a new place to live. My roommate just got engaged so she'll be moving out soon. I either need to find a new roommate or a cheaper place for just me. I'm not sure what I want to do yet. I should really decide in the next month, so I have time to find what I need before our lease is up."

"That is a tough decision. Sometimes I think it would be nice to have a roommate, someone to talk to and have fun with. I'm not home much anyway. But I really like my alone time."

"Same with me. If I did get a roommate, it would need to be with someone I really connect with. I'm leaning toward finding my own place. A new independence and freedom. Sort of empowering to be able to live alone, create my own space, and devote it to honoring myself and what I need." Maria sighed, "Well, I guess that's settled. I'll start looking for a one-bedroom apartment. I've never had my own place before."

"How exciting! You are going to love it! Let me know what specifically you are looking for and I will see what I can find too. And if you want me to go with you to look at places, let me know."

"That would be great! Now that I've made my decision, I'm feeling excited about it too. It seems like the right thing for me to do right now."

They walked a little more and came to a small waterfall. A bench had been placed there, so they sat down. "This is my favorite spot. I always stop and sit here for a while whenever I walk here," Maria admitted.

"This would be a good time for me to tell you about the dream I had this morning. It was amazing; I didn't want to wake up."

"Really! Go on, I can't wait to hear about this one!"

Lily told Maria about her dream in as much detail as she could. "The energy in the dream was so intense. And when I woke up, I was still buzzing. The feeling was still with me! Oh my God, the passion and fire, I've never imagined anything like that! I know I'm a romantic, but my imagination could not have come up with anything that powerful. I had no idea it could be like that. Do you think it's really possible for people to connect so deeply and have that kind of experience together?"

"I'm sure it's possible. I've never heard of anything like this, but that doesn't mean it doesn't exist. What do you think the dream means?"

"I don't know. I was hoping you could help me figure it out. Is it about me and Frank? Is it about me wanting something deeper in a relationship? Does it represent something else? I just don't know. What comes to you?"

"It could be all of those together. I think it is about you and Frank and the deep connection you feel with him." Maria's eyes got big as another idea hit her. "Oh! Maybe you and Frank were astral projecting and meeting on some other plane. That would be exciting! There are so many possibilities. You have been doing a lot of soul searching and personal healing and transformation. It could be something to do with that."

"Yes, anything is possible. It definitely adds to my confusion about Frank, though. The emotions and feelings were so powerful and intense. I've had fantasies before and even some really great sex dreams, but they were nothing like this!"

"Wow, it must have been a doozie!"

Lily sighed deeply and leaned over, her face in her hands. "I just don't know what to do. I feel guilty when I'm with Derrick, like I've betrayed him, even though I haven't done anything. And I don't know if this thing with Frank is even real or just a fantasy. I have no idea if he feels the same way or not. How do I deal with this? Maria, you have to help me!"

"Okay, okay! Take a breath. It seems like the priority is to find out what Frank is feeling. Once you know that you can figure out how to proceed, and eventually make a decision about Derrick."

"You're right. That makes sense. I need to talk to Frank."

"We were going to talk about Derrick this time, remember? I was going to say maybe we should skip it, but actually this might be just the right time to sort that out."

They got up and starting walking on the path again. Lily studied the path in front of them as they walked, not knowing what to say about her relationship with Derrick.

Maria sensed her reluctance. "So how have things been between you two lately?"

"Except for my distancing myself from him out of confusion and guilt, it's been fine. He's so thoughtful and sweet. He's actually been a little more romantic recently. I know he would do almost anything for me. But I'm noticing more lately that he doesn't really hear what I'm saying. It's like he has this image in his mind, and if what I say doesn't fit with that, it doesn't even register. He says he'll support whatever I decide to do, but it doesn't seem like he really means that. It's more like he'll support me in the vision he has for us."

"It does seem like the two of you are on two different wavelengths. Not really connecting."

"Exactly, sometimes it's like we are speaking different languages." She gazed out at the beauty of the park they were walking through. "We are so different. I don't think we need to do everything together or have all the same interests. I'm realizing that my spirituality is really important to me now. I do wish that he were interested in some of these spiritual topics, that we could talk about it, and he could come with me to some of these events. It would just be nice to be able to share it with him."

Maria nodded in understanding, considering all that Lily had said as they walked. "How's your sex life?"

"Uh, we don't exactly have one. He's a great kisser, and I love that, no complaints in that respect," Lily admitted self-consciously, trying to quickly cover up what she had just revealed.

Maria stopped abruptly in her tracks, her mouth dropping open. "Let me get this straight. You're in your 30's. You've been dating a gorgeous man for over a year. You say you're in love with him, but you haven't slept with him? What's up with that?"

"I know it seems crazy. I had terrible luck with men before meeting Derrick. I always felt like if I loved them enough to sleep with them that it would last forever. Well, each one proved me wrong and after the last one destroyed my heart, I made a vow to myself that I wouldn't make that mistake again, and I would wait until I was sure I was going to marry him. I'm still not sure Derrick's the one."

"So, tell me what is good about this relationship? There must be something good that keeps you with him."

"We get along really well. We have fun together. We love each other. He's a really great kisser and we have a strong physical attraction. We both enjoy being outside. We complement each other, he's good at numbers and money, while I'm good at sensing and feeling. He's more in the physical world and I'm more in the intuitive and spiritual."

"I bet he helps you to be more grounded in the present, doesn't he?"

"Yes, I guess that's true."

"The more you do in your work with energy, the more important it will be to have others around you that will help you stay grounded, and make sure you are cared for."

"Are you saying I need a man to take care of me?"

"No, not at all. I'm saying that when we spend so much

time connecting to other spirits, dimensions, etc., it is important to have ways to come back to the present and to be grounded in the physical. It doesn't have to be a man, it could be a friend, a family member, or even a pet. But it could be that this is one of the purposes for your relationship with Derrick."

"I see what you're saying. And it does make sense. I guess it is just one more piece of the puzzle to keep in mind as I try to figure this out."

"You don't have to figure it out today. Just keep an open mind and expand your awareness to see the whole picture. Keep gathering pieces of the puzzle and then see how it all comes together."

"I can do that. The first piece is still with Frank. I'm not looking forward to that conversation."

"You can do it. You say he's easy to talk to and will listen not only to your words but to your emotions and energy." Maria put her arm around her friend and gave her a gentle squeeze. "It will be fine, just do it!"

"I know, I know. I just need a little time to figure out what to say."

Maria looked into her eyes with focused intent. "Connect with your soul before you make the call and let the words flow through."

Lily nodded, recognizing the truth of what she needed to do. "Thanks, I needed that. I'm so grateful for your support. I don't know what I'd do without you."

"You're very welcome. Now you could pay me back by

setting me up with someone like Frank. Does he have any brothers or close friends like him?"

Lily laughed, "I'll see what I can do."

Chapter 22

*Oh, Soul, I really need your help. I'm trying to stay
connected to you and follow your guidance, but it is so
hard when I'm all confused about the men in my life.
What can I do to sort it all out and see everything
clearly? Please guide me as to what I should do? Please
give me the right words to say when I talk to Frank
tomorrow. Do you have any advice?*

Speak your truth. You are being guided.

*I'll do my best, please help me to tap into the necessary
strength and courage.*

~Lily's Journal

Lily and Frank had arranged to talk on Thursday
during the day, since they both were free for the day
and their conversations usually ended up lasting a
couple of hours. Even though Lily had been sitting there
waiting for the phone to ring, she was startled when it
actually did. Her stomach a tight ball of nerves, she had been
thinking for days about what to say to Frank, envisioning a

hundred different scenarios of how this conversation would go. She still wasn't sure what to say or how to say it.

"Hey there! It feels like it's been a month since we've talked, but I know it's only been a week. How are you?" The warmth of Frank's voice began to soften her nerves and was replaced with excitement and joy.

"It has been a busy week. You're right; it does feel like a month. It's so good to hear your voice again." Lily exhaled and relaxed a little more. The sound of his voice was a balm to her nerves.

"I've been doing more research, trying to get as much done as possible before the fall semester starts again. That's been taking all of my time lately."

"How is your research going?"

"I'm at a point of searching through a lot of books and articles looking for information to back up my theories. It's the most time-consuming part of the whole thing. I really enjoy the practical parts, trying out different approaches, talking to people, learning about the different beliefs and practices. That's what excites me and gets me going. But this part is the tedious, boring work. I wish I could pawn it off on some students, but I really need to do this for my own understanding so that I can write it up. I guess I could have someone look through the research for me and just pull out the good stuff, to save me some time. But my department doesn't have much of a budget for that right now, so I feel like I need to just do it."

"You may not like this part of the process, but I can tell you to love what you are doing. You light up when you talk about it. It is even apparent through the phone."

"That's true, I do love my work. I'm so grateful that I can do this and get paid for it! I really am blessed! And along those same lines, how did you feel about the long distance healing you did last time? As a teacher, I would love to hear how the experience went for you."

Anxiety filled Lily's chest and she had a hard time taking a breath, much less speaking. "Uh, it was good," was all she could squeak out.

"That's it? That's all you have to say about it?"

"It was a good experience for me, but I don't know how it was for you. What did you think?"

"I thought it was amazing! I don't think you realize how powerful your healing abilities are. This is not beginner stuff here. That was a very advanced session. I've worked with many different healers over the years, but I've never experienced a session like that long distance before."

"Really? I was just doing what you told me to do."

"Yes, but your gifts and intuition kicked in and it went beyond what I told you and you know it."

"I guess this is all so new for me that I don't know what is normal and what is beyond. I still feel pretty insecure about it. I hope we can continue to practice this so that I can feel more confident."

"I'm all for that!" He paused. "Are you sure you're alright? You seem more guarded than usual, not your normal happy self. Talk to me."

Lily took a deep breath and exhaled loudly. "I don't know how to bring this up, but I know that I need to talk to you about it." She gathered her thoughts while Frank waited patiently. "Ok, that session threw me for a loop. It was intense, more than I expected. The part that really got me was when I was pulled into it with you. I don't know if I lost my grounding or how that happened, but it probably wasn't very professional for me to join you in your healing session."

Frank chuckled. "Professional? It was a miraculous gift and you are worried about whether it was professional? I'm sorry, but I think that part was beyond our control. We were open and welcoming, and were gifted with a profoundly deep experience. It could very well be a once in a lifetime experience. I thank you for your part in it, and I also thank all the other beings that made it happen as well."

"Alright, I can accept that it was a gift from the beings that were helping. But what do you make of what happened during that other part?"

"What do you mean?"

"We were in a space of pure love, surrounded by and bathing in all that love, with all those wonderful beings around. Then we were together, you and I, connected in that loving space. What do you make of that?"

"They were blessing us with their love. I think it was a great gift, especially that we could experience it together."

"Do you think there was some kind of message there for us?"

"Maybe it is to appreciate the love that is all around us."

"Maybe," Lily responded flatly.

"What do you think the message was?"

"It just seemed like there was more to it than that. We were both experiencing the love from the beings when we were separate, but then they brought us together and we were connected. We merged together and became one. It seems like that was important, the two of us being together."

"Maybe they were just validating the connection that we have together, which we are already aware of."

Lily sighed, realizing that Frank wasn't going to admit to anything today. "That could very well be. Maybe we'll get more pieces of this puzzle with our future sessions."

"Yes, let's see what else they bring to us."

They talked for another hour about various topics, even though they had passed the initial session topic. Lily still felt like she was tied in knots. Her feelings for Frank had not died after talking to him, in fact they seemed more real than ever. He didn't seem to pick up on it, though, which made her believe that he hadn't felt anything for her during that session, only the love from the other beings. She may have missed her golden opportunity to bring it up too. Now she would have to wait for the angels to provide another one, or for them to bring more messages. Hopefully they would be crystal clear and obvious this time. *Angels, please don't let Frank wiggle out of it a second time!*

Chapter 23

Soul, I tried to talk to Frank about my feelings, but I chickened out. I broached the subject of our connection, but when he didn't seem to be going in the direction I was hoping, I let it go. I still don't seem to be seeing things very clearly. You said to speak my truth, but I have a hard time knowing what my truth is. Is my truth what is in my head? Is it what is in my heart? Is it something else?

Your truth is what you know without question, at the core of your being.

Hmm. I guess I haven't gotten to that one yet. I still have so many questions.

~Lily's Journal

Lily tossed and turned in her bed, completely tangled up in her own sheets. She finally decided it was pointless, that sleep was eluding her. She emerged from her bed to make herself some tea. A steaming cup of chamomile may be just what her spinning mind needed to finally settle down.

She sat in her recliner sipping her tea and thinking. There were too many variables that were up in the air right now for her to be able to sort anything out. An image of Serena popped into her mind. Lily realized it had been a while since she had seen her healer. Maybe a session with Serena would help her to gain some clarity. She decided she would schedule an appointment this week, the first available. With that decision, she finally started to relax. She let out a big sigh, finished her tea and then went back to bed and slept.

Serena happened to have an opening the next afternoon, right after Lily finished work. No coincidence, of course. Lily had looked forward to this session all day. It was always good to see Serena, but right now she had so much bothering her right now that she was just grateful to be here.

Serena opened the door and her warm smile and open arms touched Lily, and even while they were hugging, she felt herself letting go of some of her tension.

"Oh, Serena, I'm so glad to be here today. You have no idea."

"Tell me, what's going on?"

"I've been doing my journaling, meditating and connecting with my soul, as you've taught me, but I feel like I'm getting more confused, especially about the men in my life. I know we talked about this some the last time I was here, but it is getting more intense." She told Serena about the healing session, dreams, and thoughts and feelings about Frank.

"So, what is so confusing about this?"

"I'm still with Derrick. He's a wonderful man and I know

he wants to marry me, have kids, a nice house in the suburbs, and a cabin on a lake. A lovely picture. He is such a great guy, very kind and loving, but he doesn't share my spirituality. He doesn't get that at all. And I don't connect with him like I do with Frank. But Frank only sees me as a friend. I don't think he wants any more than that."

"I see. Close your eyes and relax for a moment. If you could look within yourself, your soul, and ask to see what your life would look like if you married Derrick, what would you see?"

Lily did as Serena suggested. "Like I said, I see us living in a house in the suburbs, with a couple kids, going to the cabin in the summers, with him working while I would stay home with the kids."

"Now look at how you would be feeling in that future. Can you connect to your feelings and emotions? Look deep within for this."

"I am happy, it is a good life, but I am not fulfilled. There is an emptiness, a longing for more."

"Ok, so are you saying that on the surface everything looks great, but looking deeper, you feel empty and unfulfilled?"

"Yes, I guess that is true. And honestly that's how I have been feeling before I came to you that first time. It's what prompted me to seek a healer. I just thought it was because of my spiritual stuff coming to the surface and needing to make decisions about my life."

"True, but if you stayed with Derrick, would you be following the urgings of your soul, or would you be staying on the same path that you have been on because it's comfortable?"

"I hadn't thought of it that way. That makes a lot of sense."

"So, looking at it this way, it is not so much choosing between the two men, but choosing which path your soul wants you to follow. The path that you are on, or a different one? Once you choose your path, you may find that one of these men is on that same path, or maybe not."

"That does seem to be a simpler way to look at it. It doesn't make the choices any easier or less painful, though."

"No, I'm sure it doesn't. You might want to keep separating out the tangles. Make decisions about your relationship with Derrick based purely on that relationship; how it feeds you, and how you feel about it deep within yourself. I know you love him, but go deeper, and see what you find. Frank has nothing to do with that, so don't let that tangle back in."

"You're right. I shouldn't stay with Derrick just because I can't have Frank. I need to find what meets my needs and makes my soul truly happy and fulfilled. I also need to let go of the picture I have had in my head of what the perfect life would look like. That image of my future with Derrick looks exactly like what my younger self always dreamed of. But I'm not a schoolgirl anymore. I want more than that now. And I need to give myself permission to want more, to know that it is ok and not selfish."

"OK, I think this may be where your healing needs to focus on today. Letting go of your old beliefs about your future, and also healing any unworthiness that doesn't let you have what you truly want."

"You nailed that one. There's something in me that thinks I don't deserve to have more, and how dare you even think you could have more than this. Oooh! That's a biggie! Let's get rid of that," Lily offered, then became puzzled as another thought came to her. "Another friend recently said that Derrick grounds me, which helps me to be able to focus my energy on my purpose and not on the menial tasks of life. If that's the case, he would be providing the basis for me to find my own fulfillment and purpose. What do you think of that?"

"That is a possibility, one that you need to spend more time clarifying with your soul to see what is true for you. One thing to check is whether his behind the scenes support helps you and empowers you toward your soul's purpose, or does it hold you back. It is possible to have someone in your life, not actively on the same spiritual path as you, but who supports you and your purpose by assisting you in the everyday. They gently push you and empower you to be your best, even if it is something they are not particularly interested in. Only you and your soul can answer that." Serena motioned to the massage table. "Why don't you lie down and we'll get started."

Lily lay down, Serena said a prayer and began gently touching Lily's feet and then moved to her shoulders. Lily felt the soft tingling energy moving through her, starting where Serena's hands touched her and then moving through her entire body. No matter how many times she experienced this, it still amazed her. She felt relaxed, with her body buzzing.

"Connect with the light in the center of your body. Breathe into that light." She paused for the span of three breaths. "Now extend that light down through your body, through the bottoms of your feet and into the earth. Feel your energy now breathing and flowing with the loving energy of the earth. Gather up this energy and allow it to move back up through your body and out the top of your head, connecting with the heavens, the universe, all that is. Then gather that loving, healing energy and bring it back down into your body to your center. You are now connected above and below to the healing energy of the universe and also to the core of your being, your soul. Take a few breaths here, and then tell me what you feel."

Lily took her breaths as instructed. "I feel relaxed. I feel connected and grounded and at peace. The light in me is bright and radiant. It feels wonderful!"

"Let's look at the belief that you are not worthy of having the life that you truly desire. Can you feel where in your body that belief is held? Even if you have to imagine it."

"This seems silly, but it feels like it is in my throat."

"That's not silly. The throat is a common place for holding, especially holding what we don't feel we can say out loud to others, what we keep quiet about, what we feel we don't have a voice about, and even what is difficult to swallow."

"I feel a warmth filling my throat, and it feels like there is a big lump that makes it hard to swallow and also hard to breathe."

"How long has this belief been held there? What's the first thought that comes to you?"

"What comes to me is an incident when I was five years old. I have an image of me doing a project for school, drawing pictures of our future self. I was going to draw myself as a doctor helping kids who were sick. Someone made a comment that I couldn't do that. Girls couldn't do that. And only really smart people can be doctors. So, I changed my drawing to be a family with two kids, a house, and a dog. I did it to fit in and be accepted." Lily became still for a few moments, then gasped. "Now I see a time when I was a peasant girl with big dreams. I knew that I was meant for much more than cleaning stables and doing laundry for others. I wanted to go to school, to learn to read and write, to help my people by becoming a doctor. I kept this to myself out of fear, because this was not something that was acceptable for girls and I didn't want to be punished for having such foolish thoughts. One day I let it slip to my brother when we were arguing, that someday when I was a doctor, he would regret being so mean to me. This simple slip caused me great pain and anguish once he told our father and then the community leader. I was beaten and told that I needed to behave like all the other girls and follow the rules and traditions. My future would be to marry the man that my father chose and have children, take care of the house and family. They told me that it would be far less painful for me to accept this path than it would be to continue these silly ideas. I was a poor girl in a small village. This was the only life that I was born to, and all that I deserved. I don't understand where this came from, I've never been a peasant, but it seems like a memory, so clear and real."

"That is a past life memory emerging. It was showing you an old pattern that has probably been with you through many lifetimes.   How did you, the peasant girl, feel when your dreams were shut down?"

"I cried for days, and when I was done I felt like an empty shell. I felt worthless. All of my dreams of greatness were crushed. Not only did I feel I wasn't good enough to do what I desired, but I didn't feel I was good enough for anything. I was unworthy of a better life, and I took that belief deep within me. There was sadness and pain with all of that, and I held that all within me, never letting anyone know how I felt."

"Now connecting with your soul and your angels around you, ask ... *Am I good enough? What do I deserve?* And wait to sense the answers."

There was a long silence before Lily responded, with tears trickling down her face. "Yes, I am good enough. I am more than good enough. I deserve anything that I can imagine. I deserve to be happy beyond my wildest dreams. I see an image of the universe opening up to me like a giant buffet, and I can have whatever I want. Wow! It feels real to me, but there is part of me that still is skeptical."

"What is that part feeling or saying?"

"That I'm fooling myself. Who do I think I am? There's anger inside, resentment."

"Is that anger and resentment a part of you? Where did it come from?"

"No, it doesn't feel like it is mine. It is what I have picked up from others. They couldn't have what they wanted, so why should I. Phew! I don't want to carry this."

"Imagine sending that back to where it came from, and also sending out love and healing, so that they can have the opportunity to heal this for themselves."

"It feels good to clear it from me, and to also help them. The lump in my throat is gone now. I can swallow normally again."

"Feel the light pouring into your throat, bringing healing, love, acceptance, worthiness. Whatever is needed for complete healing, allow it to be received."

A potent silence filled the room as the healing continued. Lily saw vibrant colors swirling thorough her body, within her closed eyes, along with gentle warmth and soothing vibrations. It may have been minutes, or hours, but time seemed to have no meaning while Lily was immersed in this healing light. She slowly came back to the present moment, her body still lightly tingling all over.

Lily giggled. "Who needs drugs or sex when you can have sessions like that! Hey, that could be a new ad campaign for you! On second thought, don't do that, I'll never get an appointment when I need one if you advertise like that!"

Serena smiled lovingly. "How do you feel?"

"I feel amazing! Like I could do anything, or maybe I'll just stay here and sleep, hoping to go back to that experience again. The beginning was good, it got into some deep things that I hadn't realized were problems. I mean I knew I had issues with worthiness, but I had no idea it went so far back or what was at the core of it. It makes so much sense when it comes to what I have been struggling with. The part about the past life pattern, was that real?"

"I believe it was. But it comes down to trusting what you sense and feel. There would be no way to prove whether it really happened or not, but does that matter? The message certainly fit with what needed healing for you."

"The message of it definitely resonated with what I needed to heal and brought me to a deeper place within myself than I would have accessed otherwise. I trust that."

She stopped to reflect on more about the session. "When the healing light came in with all the psychedelic colors, I was in some other place. I felt weightless and seemed to float in a sea of bliss. I didn't care about anything. I also felt completely loved and accepted. I sensed loving messages coming to me, I'm not sure who sent them. It was messages about how I am valued, appreciated, and loved. They also pointed out my various gifts, and ways that I am special and important to the world. I felt these messages sink into me, become part of me. It is hard to describe."

"And do you feel different now? How about your unworthiness?"

"I do feel different, though I'm not sure what it is. I don't feel my unworthiness anywhere now. I hope that means it is gone."

"Some habits may continue, and you may need to consciously remind yourself that you are different now. You are worthy of all good things. I imagine you will notice more changes as you go about the rest of your week. I look forward to hearing about it."

As Lily left she thought, *This felt like a really big and important healing for me on very deep levels. It will be interesting to see how this changes things for me, how I respond, think and feel. I wonder if my vision for the future could have changed after that session. This could be interesting.*

Chapter 24

Soul, I need your help! I feel like I'm going crazy. I'm completely obsessed with Frank and my feelings for him. I know I need to talk with him again, but I'm so afraid. He could really break my heart, and worse, I could lose the best friend I've ever had. What do I do? I'm so confused and conflicted.

Take a chance. Clarity will come.

Okay, maybe if I talk with him about my feelings everything will become clear. Thanks Soul!

~Lily's Journal

After several sleepless nights and meaningless days, Lily couldn't avoid calling Frank any longer. *"It's either call him or be locked up in the Loony Bin because I'm so obsessed that I can hardly function. I can't think of anything else. I'm making mistakes at work. I'm completely spacey. I can't get anything done. Can't even focus on a conversation. Uggh!"*

She paced around her apartment for another half hour before gathering the courage to make the call. Her hands were shaking as she held the phone. Her stomach was completely in knots. *"Wait, I think I'm going to be sick. No, you're not. You are going to make this call and put us out of your misery! Oh, alright. I'll do it."*

Frank answered the phone on the fifth ring, just when she thought it would go to voicemail. His voice caught her off guard and she struggled for what to say. "Hi, Frank. How are you?" How lame was that?

"Lily! Is everything ok? I didn't expect a call from you today."

"I know, I hope it is okay that I called. Are you busy? Do you have time to talk?"

"Yes, this is actually a pretty good time to talk. What's up?"

She took a deep breath. "Well, there is something that I've been wanting to talk to you about, but it is not easy for me. I'm not sure how to say it or how you'll react."

"Whatever it is you know I'm here for you, and I will listen with love and acceptance. I think you know you can trust me."

"Of course I trust you, that's not the problem."

"So just tell me, what is the problem?"

"Well, we both admit that we had a deep connection from the moment we met, right?"

"Right."

Lily gathered up her courage. Her thoughts spilled out in a big gush, words flying fast and furious before she could change her mind. "Well, for me it has been building and now has me all tangled up in feelings that I am trying to sort out, but I'm not very successful at it. And I'm not sure what to do about that. And I don't know if you feel the same way or if this is just me. I'm afraid that by my telling you, it may mess up our friendship, but I couldn't keep it to myself any longer."

"So, you're saying that you have feelings for me beyond friendship. Am I understanding that right?"

"Yes."

Frank paused and took a deep breath, trying to find the right words, audibly exhaling. "You are one of the most important people in my life. I deeply care about you, and your friendship means the world to me. But I really want this to stay as friendship. I'm not looking for a relationship, and don't want one at all! I think you are one of the most amazing women I have ever met, and I would be the luckiest man in the world to have you, but I just can't do this. I'm so sorry. I never wanted to hurt you. God, I feel so bad that there isn't a way to avoid hurting you right now. I hope you can believe me when I tell you that this is not about you. I'm just not at a point where I can be in any relationship. Honestly, I don't know if I will ever be. I've got a lot of healing to do before I can go there again."

Tears were rolling down Lily's face. She tried to sound accepting and grateful for his kind words. "Thanks for telling me. I appreciate your honesty. I'll let you go. We'll talk later."

"I'm so sorry, Lily. We'll get through this together, okay? Don't let this get in the way of our friendship. Call me anytime. I mean that, I am still here for you." He waited for her to respond. "Are you sure you're okay?"

"I'll be fine, don't worry about me."

"Alright then, if you're sure. I'll definitely talk to you in a couple days, if not before."

"Okay, bye." She managed to hang up before she started to bawl. Then she cried so hard her chest was convulsing. She curled up on her bed and surrendered to the tears.

"What is wrong with me? Why wouldn't he want me? Am I so unlovable? He mustn't find me attractive. We had such a deep connection on all levels that he mustn't be attracted to me physically." She cried for about an hour, cleansing herself thoroughly with tears, not to mention her pillow.

When she finally stopped crying, she got out her journal. She wrote about the conversation, her feelings, her beliefs, her assumptions, her fantasies, all of it. Then she went deeper. She called for her angels to gather all around her and connected to her soul at her core. She asked these questions again, but this time she waited for answers from her soul and angels.

Her soul said, *Look at the bigger picture.*

"What is the bigger picture? He doesn't want me."

Look deeper.

Lily replayed the conversation in her head. A faint smile crept over her face as a new realization hit her. *"Hmm. He never did say he didn't find me attractive. He never said he didn't love me. He said he couldn't be in a relationship and that he had healing to do."*

Look deeper.

Lily replayed the conversation again, but this time she approached it with a detached perspective, similar to when she did the healing session on him. She focused on his emotions and feelings as he was talking. She could feel his pain. It was painful for him to know he was hurting her, but there was also another pain behind it that caused his reaction. He sincerely felt bad about turning her down. She could feel love there. He loved her as a friend, that is definitely true. Was there more? Fear. He was afraid to go there. He was hurt so deeply years ago that he shut himself off from ever truly loving, or letting himself be that vulnerable to anyone else again. Behind the fortress protecting his heart was a deep well of pain.

"So, this really is not about me, or about him not having feelings for me. He can't let himself have feelings for me, because it would be too painful. Am I on the right track here?" Lily felt a calm peaceful feeling settle in around her. *"I'll take that as a yes. So, what do I do about this?"*

Help him heal.

"Maybe we can both do a healing session next time." Again, a deep peaceful calm filled her and she relaxed with a sigh. A knowingness that everything would be okay comforted her and allowed her to sink into a deep sleep.

The next day, Frank sent her a message asking if she was alright. It was sweet for him to check in on her. She told him she understood and was okay with that. She suggested that they both do sessions during their next call. He agreed.

Divine inspiration flowed into her in a rush. *"What if we could do a simultaneous heart healing for both of us at the same time! Would that work? We have both received healing even when we were the one facilitating it. It's perfect! And I should be the one to lead this. Am I really ready for this? Can I do this?"*

Yes, you can!

Chapter 25

Hi, Soul. I know you are giving me direction, inspiration, and guidance. I'm so grateful for all the ways you are helping me. Please help me to prepare, be ready, and have all that I need to heal myself and also to assist Frank in whatever he needs. This is all new to me, and I have lots of doubts, but please help me to follow guidance and trust that it will all work as it is meant to.

You can do it. All will be well. You are not alone.

Thanks, I'm starting to believe you!

~Lily's Journal

Lily woke in the morning with thoughts of Frank and their damaged hearts. She was still feeling the sting of rejection and heartbreak, even after understanding what was behind it. Her own dramatic spin was keeping her engaged in the pain of it rather than seeing any of the positives. She was feeling more optimistic after her soul's pep talk, but now she could feel herself sinking into her own little pity party, wallowing in sadness and despair.

"How can I get myself out of this funk so that I can help both of us to heal and move forward?"

Take time for yourself.

"I can do that, I do have the whole day off today."

Candles around the room gave it a soft glow, even in the daylight. Lily sat in her favorite chair and gazed into the flame of the candle, calling in all of her spiritual support. She felt their loving presences gather around her, and tears slowly trickled down her face.

"I really need your help right now to help me to let go of all I hold that keeps me stuck in this pain and suffering. I know I have had big expectations, fantasies, dreams, distorted beliefs, and hopes of being in a perfect soulmate relationship with someone. I realize I put all of that on Frank, and it wasn't fair to him. He is a great friend, one of the dearest friends I have ever had, and I may have ruined our friendship by attaching all of the extra baggage onto it." More tears poured down, dripping onto her shirt. *"That's the worst part, thinking that I may have lost him as a friend. Please help me to start healing this so I can begin repairing our friendship. What do I need to do?"*

Untangle.

"Okay, I need to untangle myself from Frank." Lily closed her eyes and envisioned the two of them tied together with cords of light, like yarn, all tangles and wrapped up so that neither of them could move. *"I free us both from all cords or attachments that connect us or bind us together, in any time or purpose."* She slowly began to unravel the strings and untie them. One by one they began to loosen and move. It

took quite a while, but eventually they were both free of all ties. They could both breathe and move easily now. Lily let out an exhausted sigh.

"What is next?"

Let go of your baggage.

"My baggage? Which baggage would that be? I have plenty." She pondered this for a few moments. *"It must be my old beliefs, experiences, expectations, dreams, distorted thoughts, illusions. Everything I attached to Frank, thinking he was all I ever wanted."*

She envisioned Angels gathering up all of the heavy energy of old beliefs (like not being good enough, not pretty enough, not lovable, not marriage material), and stuffing them in a tattered suitcase and taking it all away.

The next suitcase was filled with her life experiences, particularly those that had shaped her view of love, relationships, herself, all of the trauma, and even those that seemed benign. These experiences were important to making her the woman she was, but they no longer needed to be in control of her decisions or her emotions. She could take the lessons and the wisdom gained from them and let the rest go.

Other smaller bags contained her expectations, dreams, thoughts and illusions. These the angels took great care to clean and shine up first, allowing them to be seen clearly for what they were. They kept anything that was true and in alignment with her soul and taking away what no longer served her greatest good or her soul's purpose. Some of the items were more solidly attached to her, and took extra effort to detach, causing a little discomfort as they were removed. She felt lighter and freer with each release.

This was a major housecleaning. One would think a task like this would be pretty easy, but it took Lily over an hour and left her exhausted. She collapsed on her couch and didn't wake for two full hours.

Lily woke feeling much lighter and clearer. Thinking of Frank, she felt the power and depth of their friendship. This was one of the most precious connections of her life and she felt overwhelming gratitude for this gift. The other fantasies and illusions that had clouded her thinking regarding him were no longer present. It was as if the windows of her mind had been coated in a thick film of dust and dirt, and had finally been washed, leaving them crystal clear and sparkling again.

A new confidence filled her, and she knew she would be guided and supported as they embarked on the joint healing session. She felt more connected to her soul and her angels than ever before, an unexpected side benefit from her heartbreak and meltdown. She knew in her heart and soul that all would be well. She may not know the outcome, but it would all turn out for the best in the long run. She truly believed that and trusted in it completely.

This clarity and confidence did not seem to affect her nerves, however, as she prepared to call Frank for their phone session. Enormous butterflies stirred up her insides. Not as bad as before their last call, but still unsettling. Taking deep breaths, she calmed herself, called in her angels for support, and dialed the phone.

Hello there, Lily. How are you?" His simple words conveyed all of his compassion and concern for her.

"Hi, Frank. I am doing really well. The last couple of

days have been deeply healing for me. I spent the day yesterday connected with my soul and my angels in the most amazing healing energy. We cleared away a huge amount of old baggage, emotional and energetic stuff that I no longer need, and also let go of beliefs, expectations and attachments that were no longer true for me. I have changed so much in the last year, and there was a lot that needed to shift within me to be in sync with that. Does that make sense?"

"It makes perfect sense."

"I can see how much those things had distorted my views and thoughts about you and our relationship. It had become distorted by all of those old outdated ideas. By clearing out all of that, I have a clarity that I never imagined. I hadn't realized how messed up it all was until after it was repaired. It's amazing that you don't realize how things really are when you are immersed in the depths of the struggle."

"So, what do you see differently?"

"I hope you don't take this the wrong way. I don't mean for it to sound harsh, but I don't know how else to say it. I see our connection as a friendship that is deep and true, across all time and space. If you had decided you could no longer be in contact with me, I would miss your friendship, but I know the soul connection will always be there. It doesn't matter if I never see you again. It feels that strong and true to me. I realize it is a precious gift that I will always treasure, and nothing will ever take that away. I need nothing else from you than that. You could say goodbye to me right now and I would be okay."

"Wow! You really have done a lot of work in a short amount of time."

"I realized that I wasn't really in love with you, but was caught up in the illusion and fantasy of it. I was nervous to talk to you today, afraid that it would all come back, but I feel perfectly clear. I'm so happy about that!"

"I must say, I am amazed! I expected this to be so much more difficult and awkward. I'm happy that this experience was able to catalyze such a deep healing for you. That is so great! And what a wonderful validation for you to know that you can do this for yourself when you need it."

"It really has taught me a lot!"

"This has brought my issues to the forefront of my mind as well, showing me what I still need to heal. So, thank you for that. I feel so bad for causing you pain, but now I see that sometimes that is the best way to get things cleared away for the deepest healing. You are incredibly brave for expressing your feelings and then going after all your old issues instead of allowing them to go back into hiding. Keeping them hidden is a cop-out, and I admit that's what I have been doing for too long. I'm in awe of you, your courage, and your resilience. You are truly amazing!"

"Thank you for that. I am so grateful for you!"

"You mentioned that you might want to do a joint healing of some kind today. Do you still want to try that? Or have you had enough healing already?"

"I definitely want to try it if you are game. I feel like I am in a good space for it now. This will be a good challenge. I received the inspiration for it, but I'm not sure how it will go. I'm trusting that we will be guided."

"I have no doubt. I think this will be fun. I've never tried anything like this, but since we have both received healing from the sessions we've done together, it doesn't seem like much of a stretch. How will we start?"

"We say a prayer to seal the space and call in all beings of light who are to assist us in this healing. We ask that they protect us and guide us for our greatest and highest good. We both open ourselves up to receive healing energy and guidance as needed for our individual healing and to support each other. Then we each state our intentions for what we want to receive. My intention is for deep healing of my heart, and all levels of my being that have been hurt or locked down to avoid pain, from all time."

"That's beautiful. My intention is similar, so I will use yours but also add that I want to break down the walls that I have put up around my heart, to bring deep healing of my old pains and to allow love to come in."

"Now we both take deep breaths and connect to the divine beings around us. Allowing ourselves to sink into a space of allowing and receiving, open to the guidance and healing that is coming through for our greatest good."

They both sat with eyes closed. Lily had her phone on speaker and Frank had his headphones on. Both suddenly became aware of a light surrounding them, the room seemed to be filled with light. It was peaceful, gentle and inviting. They were being lifted and transported to another place, a special dimension for healing the heart. It felt similar to the loving place they were in for their last session, but the colors were different, swirling greens, blues, and pinks. The feeling was one of complete support, acceptance, and compassion. They were each lying on separate tables. Beings of light surrounded both of them and were busily removing items from their energy fields. Clearing debris from all over their bodies.

Frank felt like there was surgery going on to remove the walls he had in place. Some of it was being chipped away meticulously, while other areas were being blasted apart. He hadn't realized how thick his barriers had become. As they removed a piece, the area was immediately filled with light to heal what was underneath. They worked as a well-orchestrated team, efficiently and seamlessly.

Lily felt every part of her being getting a thorough cleaning and cleansing. The beings were careful to clear away even the tiniest speck of darkness from every nook and cranny in every cell. She was filled with light and love as golden healing energy flowed through her.

Though both Lily and Frank were receiving simultaneous healings, time was meaningless, allowing them both to receive exactly what they needed, as if they had all the time in the world. Once the individual parts were complete, they drifted to another beautiful, peaceful realm. This place had the sharpest vibrant colors, more so than any seen on earth. Bright green foliage grew alongside a deep turquoise stream, with a breathtaking waterfall surrounded by exotic flowers of all colors. They were guided to step into the stream to be bathed and cleansed by the crystal-clear waters. The water was not only the perfect temperature, but it had a different consistency to it. It didn't feel wet. They could swim through it easily and comfortably, weightless and without effort. Healing light shimmered within the water, glowing all around them. It was soothing to their body, mind, heart and soul, a balm for all that had been healed. Upon emerging from the water, they were completely dry, clean and clear, inside and out.

Light beings led them to a sacred space behind the waterfall. It was safe and sheltered and filled with silvery light. As Lily and Frank sat in the middle, the beings formed a circle around them. Sound began to hum all around in soft gentle tones. Their consciousness began to shift, almost dreamlike and then they felt themselves floating in the center of the group. Love pulsed all around them, radiating from the light beings to completely encompass Lily and Frank, holding them in a bubble of love.

Inside the bubble, Lily and Frank felt complete serenity, suspended in light and love. Nothing else in the world mattered. They were at peace within themselves, feeling completely whole, healed, and fulfilled.

At the same moment, they became aware of each other. A frisson of recognition, understanding, and unconditional love passed between them. Their friendship had now been blessed in this sacred space. They knew that they would remain a part of each other no matter what happened, no matter how far they were apart, or how much time passed. Their hands were clasped together in unity as they travelled back to the earth plane.

The beings of light gave them each a private message. Lily heard a voice say, *You have all the answers within you, trust yourself. We are always with you. We love you and are so proud of you. Continue moving forward on your path. All your soul's desires will be fulfilled. All will be well.*

Frank also received a message. *You have so much love within you. Allow yourself to give and receive love and your life will be one rich with abundance beyond your wildest dreams. You deserve all happiness. Receive all the gifts that are around you. Know you are loved.*

They were gently and gracefully brought back to the present, feeling blessed and grateful for all that had been received. They both sat quietly for a few moments before breaking the sacredness of the silence.

A long sigh escaped Lily's lips. "Oh my gosh. I don't think I can speak or form coherent sentences. I honestly have no words."

"Yeah. I'm glad I don't have to go anywhere because I may be on this couch for the rest of the day and night. That was unbelievable! I think I just received about 30 years of therapy in 90 minutes. I feel like a different person. I truthfully don't know how to explain how I feel or what I experienced. It was so profound."

"It seemed to me like we each had our own separate experience for our personal healing, and when that was done, we shared each other's experiences. Is that how you perceived it as well?"

"Yes, that seems right. My personal healing was so intense and powerful that while that was happening I felt like I was being taken apart piece by piece and put back together again. I feel like a brand-new version of myself! Then when we were together, I felt sublime, like we were both being rewarded for the work we had just completed. It was paradise!"

"It really was paradise! The setting, the colors, the smells, senses, everything was incredible! And so much love for us both, they were bathing us in love!" Lily's joy emanated from her words, unable to be contained. "And when we turned to face each other in the bubble ... I don't know if I can describe what I felt in that moment. Can you describe that?"

"It was a new depth of love between us, a soul love, beyond anything I've ever experienced or even read about. It had nothing to do with sex or attraction or our human ideas. It was beyond this lifetime and this existence. Oh, I just got this, it was a reunion or remembrance of the connection we had before. That is why we recognized each other when we met. Our souls have always had this connection and always will, no matter what time or distance separates us we will always be a part of each other."

"One of the things that amazes me about this is that we both know that it is absolutely true. There is no questioning it."

"The fact that we both experienced it simultaneously, and received that knowledge together, will allow us to be able to support each other and remind each other of this truth during times when doubts or distortions come in, as I'm sure they will at some point."

"You're right. That will be important, I'm sure." Lily took a drink of water. "The healing portion for me was a continuation of the work that was started a couple days ago. It feels really good to have it almost complete. I feel more settled. How about you?"

"I'd say mine was supercharged. Like this was the moment they've been anticipating for years and they wanted to make the most of it. I have to admit, some of it was brutal! I really felt beat up, like I had been put through the meat grinder, and there was hardly anything left of me." A big loud sigh from them both was followed by laughter. "I'm so grateful they were able to put Humpty Dumpty back together again. I'm happy to say this feels like a new and improved version, and I like it!"

"What feels different to you from your old version?"

"It's weird. I feel happy, joyful, free. Like I can do anything. All of my limitations have been removed. The world is brighter, lighter, and more colorful. I'm excited for whatever is to come."

"I'm so happy for you! What a wonderful gift, to have a bright shiny new life!"

Franks voice quieted. "And I'm grateful that you were there with me. I felt your presence, even when we were experiencing separate healings, and it gave me comfort to know you were there. And I'm also grateful to know that wherever we are in the world or elsewhere, we will always support each other on the soul level. I think that is the greatest gift!"

"Stop, you're going to make me cry!" A tear of joy slipped out from the corner of her eye, but he couldn't see it through the phone. "I completely agree. We are lucky to receive such gifts. It really blows my mind."

"My mind has been blown many times already! No wonder I can't think straight. I hope my brain starts to work again before I go back to school and have to actually teach."

"All these unbelievable gifts we are being given ... it makes me wonder why they are given to us? Is there some bigger purpose or plan that we are not aware of?"

"I'm sure there is. On a soul level we agreed to whatever that is before we came into these lives. It will be fun seeing how this all plays out, won't it?"

"One surprise after another! As long as they are as good

as this, I say keep 'em coming!" Lily laughed.

They conversed further for a while about what was happening in their everyday lives. Frank suddenly had an idea, "Summer is almost over for me. It would be fun to spend some time together before I go back to school. Would you like to come up here and visit me the next time you have a couple days off?"

"I would love it! That will be so much fun!"

"Just let me know when, my schedule is pretty flexible for the next couple weeks. And you are welcome to stay here, I have plenty of room, so you don't have to stay in a hotel. If that is ok with you."

"Sounds perfect! I'll have to check my schedule and get back to you. I'll text you the dates. I'm so excited! It will be so great to see you again!"

"I'm excited too! There's lots to do and see around here. This will be great!"

"Yay! I can't wait! I'll text you as soon as I can, and we'll talk again soon! As much as I'd love to keep talking to you, I should go. Bye, Frank!"

"Later, Lily."

Lily sat in a dreamy trance for a while after hanging up. The session had been amazing. Something had shifted with her and Frank as well. She couldn't believe that he asked her to visit. This would prove whether she truly has gotten over her previous fantasies or not. Her excitement to see Frank again was already building. She wanted to see where he lived, and what he liked to do, maybe even meet his kids. This would be a great way for them to get to know each other better. The gifts kept coming!

Chapter 26

Dear Soul, that joint session with Frank was the most incredible experience of my life! I received so many wonderful gifts in that session. I feel like a different person. My obsession is gone, my thoughts are clear, my confusion has vanished. I feel fantastic! I am so grateful! I thank all those who assisted in that session in any way. I still can't believe all that I experienced. Blew my mind! I can give myself credit for being open and following the signs as they came. I know I have come a long way in the last few months. Thanks for all you've taught me!

You've done well. So proud of you!

~Lily's Journal

The next day Lily checked her schedule at work and texted Frank. "I have next Wednesday and Thursday off. Would that work for you? If not, I can try to switch with someone."

Frank responded, "Those days are perfect for me. Come Tuesday night after work. Can't wait to see you!"

Lily was so excited about her visit to Frank, her day just flew by. She worked the next five days until then, which made the time go faster. She also had a concert to attend with Maria on Saturday night, and a visit to her grandma on Sunday evening. Her schedule was so full she hardly had time to do laundry and plan what she would bring. *"Oh, I need to give something to my host. What sort of gift should I bring for Frank? Maybe a crystal from the rock shop. I'll stop there after work on Monday to see what jumps out at me, or seems appropriate for Frank."*

Derrick called to ask when they could see each other.

"I'm sorry, but I don't think it's possible this week. I work all weekend, and have plans in the evening on Saturday and Sunday. Wednesday and Thursday, I'm going to visit a friend in Duluth for a couple days. We could plan something for next weekend."

"What friend are you visiting?"

"Someone I met in the healing class I took. We've been in contact over the phone and email since the class, and have become good friends. It will be fun to get together again in person."

"Alright, I guess I'll have to wait until next weekend. I hate being apart from you and not seeing you for such long periods. I miss you!"

"I know, and I'm sorry. My schedule stinks sometimes, that's a big downside to nursing, one of the things I will not be missing when I change careers. Anyway, I'll make it up to you next weekend. Are you free on Friday night? I can come over right after work."

"I'd like that. I'll see you on Friday. Be careful on your

trip. I love you!"

"I'll be careful, don't worry. I love you too. I'll talk to you soon."

Lily felt bad about not finding time for Derrick, but she knew she wouldn't be able to focus on him when she was so excited about seeing Frank. She probably should have told him who she was going to see, but she figured he wouldn't understand. He would assume it was romantic, and get jealous, or worse, get upset and tell her not to go. She didn't want to deal with any of that right now. They usually only saw each other on the weekends anyway. They would miss this weekend, but they would see each other next weekend. Why did she feel so guilty then?

The concert was a good diversion. The music was fantastic, and it was always fun to hang out with Maria. "I'm so glad you invited me to join you. This is exactly what I needed right now," Lily commented as they lounged in a coffee shop near the concert hall.

"So, fill me in on all that has been happening with you lately. I feel like we haven't talked in ages."

Lily gave her the synopsis of what had transpired between her and Frank, the confession, healing, the shift in their friendship, and now the upcoming visit. "Wow, that is a lot to go through in a short period of time. You definitely seem to be on a fast track of spiritual transformation. How do you feel about what's going on?"

"Well, I am blown away, I am excited, I am scared to death, I am grateful ... there is just so much to process, to think about, to understand. With it happening so fast, I know I am going with the flow and following my intuition, which is good, but it doesn't give me time to take it in and really understand the messages for myself and how they fit in my current life. It feels like what is happening with Frank is really important for me. I'm not sure why or what it means yet. But I believe it will become clear soon."

"So, are you really ok with just being friends with him, right after admitting you have serious feelings for the guy?"

"I expected that would be difficult, but after the healings I have had, I'm telling you honestly those romantic feelings are no longer there. I don't know where they went, but when we spoke the other day and were in that intense session together, nothing got triggered. But the soul connection and friendship felt more solid than ever. I have no doubt that we will enjoy spending time together. I am really looking forward to it!"

"That is amazing! I can't wait to hear all about it when you get back."

"I'll definitely call you as soon as I return, maybe even from the road. It is a two-hour drive."

"And how are things with Derrick?"

"We haven't seen as much of each other lately. Part of it is because of our schedules, but also because I was so conflicted about Frank that I was keeping my distance as I tried to figure it out, and to do my own inner work. And now this week, I'm so excited about my trip that I didn't really want to see Derrick. I don't want him to know I'm going to visit a man, even as a friend. I could see him being jealous or upset, and I just didn't want to deal with that right now. Is that bad? What do you think?"

"Hmm. That's a tough one. I think most men would be

upset to know their woman was going to spend two days and nights with another man, even if they know he's just a friend. Even if he trusts you, he probably wouldn't trust the man not to put the moves on you. He may also be hurt or threatened that you are such close friends with a man other than him. He'll also be upset to find out about it later."

"You're right. I guess I'd rather fight about it later, than to get into it now and again later. Isn't there some saying about it being better to ask forgiveness than to ask permission?"

"Ha! Yeah, I think I've heard that one before. Good luck with that!"

"We are always talking about my love life. What's going on in yours?"

"The reason we always talk about yours is because you have one. Mine doesn't exist. I just haven't been able to meet any good men that really interest me lately. I guess I'm getting pickier. I used to go out with anyone I found attractive, and who seemed fun. Now, I don't want to waste my time on a date with whom I don't have anything in common, or I know won't understand me."

"How do you know they won't understand you, unless you give them a chance?"

"You're right, but that's why I'm in such a rut about dating. I want to find someone like your Frank. Hey, now that you two are just friends, maybe you can introduce me!"

"I would love to have my two favorite people get together! It would be so much fun to hang out with both of you! Maybe the next time he has a break from school he can come down here."

"Sounds good to me."

"You should take more spiritual classes yourself to meet men that have similar interests."

"I know, I really should do that. I'll keep my eyes open for something that looks good or piques my curiosity."

"Let me know what you find. I'd love to go to another class. I just can't seem to get enough of this stuff now. I think I'm becoming a spirituality junkie. I need a class to get my fix."

"No kidding. That is so true. Once you get started on this path, it becomes your whole life. That is precisely why I want to find a man who shares the same obsession. That is my primary intention. It is also my intention to get some of that fresh strawberry pie. "

"Smart woman. I like how you think! And being the good friend that I am, I will get a piece too, just to be supportive."

Maria laughed. "You are such a good friend! What would I ever do without you!"

They ate their pie, drank tea, talked and laughed until well after midnight. Lily was having such a good time she almost forgot that she had to get up early for work the next morning. "Oh my gosh, I didn't realize how late it was. I need to go home and get some sleep. This was such a great night! Thank you so much! I promise I'll call you after my trip."

"You better, I can't wait to hear all about it!" Maria called out as Lily rushed off to her car.

Chapter 27

Soul, I have a really good feeling about visiting Frank. It
feels to me like everything is lining up for this to happen. I
feel grounded and centered, and when I think about this
trip it just feels right. Am I paying attention to the right
things here? Is this an accurate interpretation?

I feel a warm, calm and cozy feeling, happy and content.
I'll take that as a yes!

~Lily's Journal

The drive to Duluth was picturesque, as it wound
around through tall pine trees along the rocky shore
of Lake Superior. The sun was just starting to set as
she arrived at Frank's house overlooking the lake. It was a
lovely log cabin-style home, with a loft upstairs overlooking
the living room and fireplace below. The exterior was a
beautiful combination of cedar and stone, in keeping with the
natural landscape. Nestled among pines and birch trees, it
embodied peace and tranquility.

Frank rushed out the front door as she got out of her car.

"Hey! You made it! I'm so excited to have you here!" He wrapped her up in a big bear hug.

"Wow, Frank, this place is gorgeous! You never told me you lived in a place like this. What a view! And you wake up to this every day?"

"I am blessed, and I am grateful for it every day. Come on in, I'll show you around." Lily grabbed her bag and followed him in.

They entered the back of the house into the main living area. The open floor plan included a kitchen and living room, with a stone fireplace on the left and two-story windows on the end, giving a breathtaking view of the lake. There was lots of natural wood and stone throughout. It felt very homey, earthy and close to nature. Even though it was a large and spacious home, there was nothing flashy or ostentatious about it. Lily paused to take it all in. A sigh escaped her lips as she thought to herself, *Oh, I could definitely see myself living here! I mean, in a place like this. Wouldn't it be heavenly?* She was brought back to the present as Frank led her to the next room.

The master bedroom was on the right, and was magnificent and masculine. It definitely seemed like Frank. The kids' rooms were on the other side of the kitchen. "We'll just skip those, pretending they don't exist, since I have no idea what state those rooms are in right now. Teenagers." He laughed, and Lily nodded in understanding. Upstairs held a loft that overlooked the main living area and the spectacular view of Lake Superior. There were also small rooms on each side of the loft; one was Frank's office and the other was storage.

"I'm sorry we don't have a dedicated guest room, but you

can have your pick of the futon in my office, or there's a futon and pull out couch in the loft. If you want to sleep in, you may want to take the office, the morning sun is very bright in the loft since it faces east."

"I'll take the office then. I probably won't sleep real late, but you never know."

"My kids are here tonight, but they will be going to their mom's tomorrow."

"I'd love to meet them."

The teenagers were watching TV, not even noticing that anyone else was in the room. "Hey! We have company. I'd like to introduce you to my friend Lily, she lives in Minneapolis. Lily, this is Sam and Sasha." They got up and shook Lily's hand.

"It's nice to meet you both." Lily smiled warmly as she greeted them.

Her first impression was that they were good kids, polite and considerate. They definitely looked like twins, but had their differences as well. Sam was the image of his father, tall and muscular with dark hair, dark eyes, and a perfectly placed dimple when he smiled. Future lady killer, was all Lily could think. Sasha had exotic light blue eyes in contrast to her long black hair with gentle waves cascading down her back. "Frank must have his hands full keeping the boys away from her," she thought. She was already a beauty, but in a few years she would be stunning.

"Nice to meet you too. So, are you my dad's girlfriend?" Sam asked bluntly.

Lily laughed. "No, sorry, we're just friends," she answered, hoping the color of her cheeks didn't deceive her.

"So, what do you like to do for fun in the summer?"

Sasha answered, "I like to ride horses. That's my favorite thing to do. I also like to draw, but I do that all year. And I like to swim and kayak in the summer."

"How about you, Sam? What do you like to do?"

"I like all sports. Mostly shooting hoops or playing baseball. I ride mountain bikes on trails, I guess that's what I do the most in the summer."

"I've never been here before. What are the best things to do around here for a tourist like me? What do you recommend?"

They both seemed to be thinking about this question. "Most people go to Canal Park to watch the ships come in and the bridge go up and down. Split Rock Lighthouse is also popular," Sam offered.

"I prefer the nature trails, there are lots of places to hike or picnic. You can travel through the woods, or along the coast. There are waterfalls, too. That's what I would recommend," suggested Sasha.

"I like that idea! I guess I'm not a typical tourist; I prefer places where there are not a lot of other people around. I love to spend time in nature, take pictures, relax. But I would like to see the bridge and the lighthouse, too. I bet I could get some great pictures there! Thanks for the awesome suggestions."

"That gives us lots of possibilities for tomorrow. Would you like some lemonade or water?" Frank offered as he led her to the kitchen.

"Lemonade sounds great."

"We made some cookies today. Would you like one?"

CHAPTER TWENTY-SEVEN

A shout came from the other room. "Who made cookies?"

"Alright, busted! Sasha made the cookies."

"If Sasha made them, then I definitely need to have one. They look delicious!" Lily chose a cookie from the plate and took a bite. "Mmmm. Sasha, oh my god. This is incredible! This has to be one of the best cookies I've ever tasted! And Snickerdoodles have always been my favorite. How did you learn to do this?"

"I work in a restaurant, and the owner makes really good food, especially the baked goods. She showed me how to make some of it, which I then try at home." Sasha beamed with pride.

"Frank, you've got it made, you have your own personal baker here. How are you not 500 pounds?"

"I'm practicing self-control. And we give a lot of it away to the friends and neighbors too." Frank chuckled, his pride in his daughter radiating from his smile.

"So, Sam, what's your hidden talent?" Lily asked.

Sam just shrugged, but his dad couldn't pass up the opportunity to brag about him. "Sam is a builder and a fixer. If anything needs to be put together, fixed or figured out, in order to get it to work, Sam's our man! They are both handy to have around, most of the time." He lovingly elbowed them as they tried to sneak by for cookies.

"Dad, you'd be lost without us," Sam teased.

"You're right, it's sad but true."

"Yeah, when he's writing or researching, he forgets to eat. He'll be in his room all day and we'll have to go in and yank him out so he doesn't starve."

"I think you exaggerate just a little.

"Not really. I bet if we weren't here, you would be working so much that you'd look like a skeleton with a really long beard, and the neighbors would be warning their kids to stay away from you."

"Ha, ha. You guys are really funny. You can go back to watching TV now."

"No way, we like talking to Lily."

Lily leaned over towards the kids. "What else can you tell me about your dad? This is fun!" She was really enjoying this time with his family. The twins were a lot of fun and they were also sweet. They teased their dad and each other, with obvious love and respect. They asked her a lot of questions, too. She could tell they wanted to know more about her and were trying to figure out what her relationship was with their dad, and why she was staying there. Did they do this with all the women he brought to the house?

Eventually the kids went off to their rooms, while Lily and Frank took their drinks out onto the porch. The steady crashing of waves against the rocky shore made for peaceful background music as they sat and soaked it all in.

"Your kids are great! They're a lot of fun. But I can tell they were putting me to the test. I hope I did okay."

"They didn't throw you over the cliff, so I'd say you're safe."

"Have they thrown others overboard?" Lily asked.

"What others?"

"The other women you've dated or brought to meet your kids."

"I've always been really protective and careful to keep

my kids away from my dates. I was never interested in a relationship, so I never wanted to introduce anyone to my kids and have them hurt when it didn't work out or have anyone use my kids to get at me. That's why they are so eager to figure out what's going on between us. Even though we are not dating, this friendship, this relationship feels different for me. I know that I can trust you completely. And I want you to know my kids and them to know you, since you are all important to me."

Lily choked up a little with that admission. "Thank you. That means a lot to me to hear you say that. I'm honored to be a part of your life like that, and I'm so happy to be here."

"I'm glad you are here too. It is one thing to talk on the phone, but it is different to be together in person. I think we'll get to know much more about each other this way."

"Yes, especially with the help of those two in there. I definitely learn a lot more about you when they are around."

"Ha! That's exactly why they are going away tomorrow!" Frank joked. They talked until Lily began to stifle a yawn. "I'm sorry, I shouldn't keep you up so late. I forgot that you worked all day and then drove all the way here. You must be ready to collapse. I'll show you your room."

Frank guided her to the office upstairs. It was a simple room, decorated with a log futon, desk and chair. Like the master bedroom, it had a masculine feel but was simple and tidy. She could tell this was Frank's space. She immediately felt comfortable and at home here. They said good night and Lily was out before her head hit the pillow.

Chapter 28

It feels so comfortable being here with Frank in his home
with his family. I expected it to be awkward, but it's the
opposite. After going through all of that with him over the
phone, we seem to have established a deeper level of trust
and can just be ourselves, without any of the usual
pretenses. And since we have already gotten past any ideas
about a physical relationship, we can relax and enjoy each
other. It feels really good! Help me to stay in the present,
with no worries or expectations, and savor the gift of these
couple days with my dearest friend.

~Lily's journal

The enticing aroma of bacon cooking roused Lily from
her sleep. She had slept so deeply, she didn't think
she moved all night. She slowly dressed and made
her way downstairs to the kitchen. There she found Sasha
flipping French toast on a griddle, Frank tending bacon at the
stove, and Sam setting out the plates, glasses, and silverware.

"Good morning! I hope we didn't wake you," Frank
cheerfully greeted her.

"I didn't hear anything, but the irresistible smell of bacon cooking got my attention. I didn't mean to sleep so late, but I think I died as soon as I laid down." She looked around the kitchen. "This all looks terrific. I didn't expect all this. Best bed and breakfast I've ever been to!"

Frank laughed, "You mustn't get out much then. But we are happy to serve you!"

They sat down to eat together. It was very comfortable and the conversation was easy. "So, what do you kids have planned for today?"

"Dad will drop us off at Mom's in a little while. I'm going to my riding lesson and will spend the afternoon at the stables."

"I'll hang out with a buddy of mine, we may bike to some trails that we like, or go swimming if it's hot. There's an outdoor pool near his house."

"You don't swim in the lake?" Lily asked.

"We sometimes take a quick dip on really hot days, but most of the time it is way too cold. It's better to swim in a pool warm enough to swim without needing a wetsuit."

"That sounds like fun. It looks like a perfect day for that, too," commented Lily.

"What are you guys gonna do?" Sasha asked.

"We haven't talked about it yet. We could drive around to see some sights. We could do some hiking. Maybe hang around here, walk along the beach and collect rocks. Depends on what Lily wants to do," Frank casually suggested.

"I'm open to anything. I love being outside, whether it's walking, hiking, or just sitting and watching the waves come in. In fact, all of those ideas sound good to me."

"Maybe we'll start with showing you what is here in the area, so you can get a better sense of where we live, since it was almost dark when you got here." Frank began picking up dishes as he spoke.

"You're right. That would be a great place to start." Lily stood up to help him clean the kitchen.

"As soon as you kids are ready, I'll take you over so we can all get going on our day." The kids took advantage of the opportunity to avoid doing the dishes and rushed off to get ready for the day.

Lily sat on the patio with a cup of coffee while Frank deposited his children at their mom's house. The view was breathtaking, but she imagined it would be even better if she had gotten up early enough to see the sun rise over the lake. Maybe tomorrow. This was her first visit to Lake Superior. She had been to other lakes, rivers and oceans, but this lake was unique. It looked like the ocean, as she was unable to see across to the other side, and the waves came in like ocean waves, but it didn't have tides like oceans do. The lake was also freshwater like most other lakes, not salt water like an ocean. She thought it would be fun to walk down there and wade in to see how cold it was, since Sam said most people didn't swim in it.

Just as she was thinking that, Frank reappeared and asked, "How would you like to take a walk along the shore?"

Lily smiled. "You read my mind. That's exactly what I was thinking about doing. I can hear the lake calling me."

"It called to me too, that's why I bought this place. I came out to visit a friend and saw the land for sale. I got out and walked around and instantly fell in love with the place. I had the house built just for us. I'm so happy with how it turned out."

"There is a lot of you in the house, but it is also connected to nature."

"I'm so glad you picked up on that. My intention was to create a warm and cozy family place that was tied in to the lake and the natural energy around us." They walked from the patio toward the lake, down steep wooden steps to the shore.

"It's so beautiful here. I can't imagine waking up to this every day."

"I know. It doesn't get old. I've lived here for over ten years now, and I am still grateful every day for the gift of living here. Growing up in inter-city Chicago, I never imagined I would ever live someplace like this, or that I could be happy being out of the city. But now when I'm in the city, I feel so cramped and overstimulated. I can't wait to get back home to this peace and tranquility. It is home to me now."

"I still live in the city, and even though I like where I live, I crave nature, trees and water. The city has many conveniences, everything you want or need is close by, but I'd leave it in a heartbeat to live somewhere like this."

"I had already been studying meditation and spirituality for many years before I came here, but all of my practices deepened when I connected with the lake, rocks and trees of this place. Other people would think this was weird, but it felt like this was where my soul belonged, and I felt guided to come here. It's where I belong."

"I totally get that. I haven't found where I belong yet, but I feel like I'm getting closer."

They walked along the shore, which was covered in smooth round rocks. "These rocks are really cool. Why are they all like this?"

"They are smoothed and shaped by the constant motion of the waves, and the friction of rubbing against the other rocks. All along the shore they look like this, one of the landmarks of the North Shore."

Frank picked one that fit in his hand and was rounded and flat. He tossed it across the water with a sidearm throw, skipping it across the waves. "Six skips, I'll have to tell Sam. Our record is nine."

"Impressive!" Lily gave it a try and hers skipped just twice. "I guess I'm a little rusty in my rock skipping."

"I've had years of practice. I used to spend hours out here with Sam and Sasha. They never want to quit until they get a really good one."

"They are great kids. I see a lot of you in them, in their looks and their kindness and presence, even at so young an age. I'm glad I got to meet them. It was fun to see the three of you together."

"Thank you. They were on their best behavior. I made some pretty big threats before you got here." Frank smiled broadly.

"Oh, come on, I don't believe that."

"It's true, but they really are good kids. They are the best thing in my life, I'm so blessed to be their dad." His pride in his kids was shining in his eyes.

Lily sat down on a large boulder at the edge of the water. She removed her sandals and stepped into the water. "Whoa! This really is cold. I didn't expect it to be so different from other lakes I've been in. I guess I won't be going swimming."

Frank chuckled. "Yeah, there are people who swim here, but most have a wetsuit if they are going to be in for a prolonged period of time. There are some little inlets that are shallow and warm up by the sun so you can wade in a little more comfortably, at least by the end of the summer. The lake as a whole is just too big to warm up, though, and by the end of summer it may get up to 60 degrees F, but in the winter it is down to 35 degrees. In the winter, most of it is covered in ice. I should show you some photos I have of the ice formations on the shore. It's spectacular!"

"I'd love to see those. I've seen waterfalls in winter and they are stunning!"

They sat on the boulders, letting the sun's warmth seep back into Lily's frozen feet. They were comfortable talking or sitting in silence, enjoying each other's company and also the natural splendor around them.

Frank seemed to be pondering a decision, then softly added, "If you like waterfalls, there is one not too far from here, it is on private property so there won't be any tourists. It's not as big and flashy as some of the others, but I find it just as striking in its own way."

"I'd love to see your private waterfall."

"It's not mine, but it is my favorite. It's a bit of a hike to get to, but it's worth it. We can pack a bag with some food and drinks. How does that sound?"

"Fantastic!"

They climbed back up to the house. Frank began gathering items to pack for lunch and stowed them in a backpack. Lily changed into hiking shoes and layered her clothes, since it was cool now by the water, but would be warmer in the sun away from the shore.

They drove a couple miles further, where Frank pulled over on the side of the road, halfway into the ditch. He pointed to a break in the trees, saying, "That's where the trail begins."

"Seriously? How did you ever find this place?"

"A friend, who had lived here all his life, brought me here. His family owns this land, so it is off limits to others." He pointed to the No Trespassing sign. "But he gave me permission to come here whenever I like."

The trail was a narrow dirt path, not groomed like the public trails, but fairly easy to follow. It wound through trees and hills, around a pond, and along a babbling stream. Most of the path was shaded and cool, which was a blessing since there was no breeze and the temperature was at least 10-15 degrees warmer away from the lake.

Lily was sweating as she trudged along the trail. She liked walking and hiking, but was not used to this hilly terrain. She hoped they would arrive at their destination before she had to ask for a breather. She sipped her water bottle to keep hydrated.

After about an hour of hiking, they reached a canyon. It was cool and shady here. Frank sat on a log and took a long drag on his water. This part of the trail had a mystical feel. Bright green moss grew on everything, the trees the rocks, even the ground seemed to be painted with this otherworldly green. Lily imagined this to be a haven for fairies. The energy of this spot pulsed with excitement. After sitting there for just a couple minutes she felt rejuvenated and ready to continue on.

Lily heard the waterfall before she could see it, and knew they were close. The path had brought them to a point that was in the middle, allowing them to go down to get to the river, or climb up to reach the top of the falls. Her camera began firing off shots in all directions.

"We can go either way, but I think the best view is from the base."

"Let's go down there then." Lily was like a little kid on a new adventure, excited about every little thing she saw.

When they reached the bottom, Frank perched himself on a big rock at water's edge. "Coming here really helps me to regain a perspective on life and connect with all the divine wonder all around me. I think it would be impossible to be in this place and not feel the presence of God. I often come here to think, to get answers, to receive guidance. I consider it one of my sacred places."

"I can see why. It's like we're in another world here, nothing else exists. And it does feel sacred. We are surrounded by light beings here. Can you feel them?"

"I feel supported, and even though I've never seen another person here, I've never felt alone here. It's very special."

"Do you bring your kids here?"

"No, actually I haven't. Since I like to come here when I want to have time to myself, to be in solitude, I've never brought anyone else here."

"So why did you bring me?"

"I knew you would appreciate it, and show it the

reverence it deserves. Also, I thought that since I felt the divine here and the potent energy, you might too. I was curious to find out what you would feel or experience here."

Lily was touched that he would share this with her. He seemed to be showing her the things that were most important to him. She was aware of the vulnerability that he was risking here with her. Neither one of them was used to sharing their special places or secrets with anyone else. She would have to do the same with him. Surprisingly that didn't feel scary or intimidating, just intriguing as to what she could share.

They each found a place to sit in meditative silence, connecting with the energy of the wondrous place and receiving all that was available in this moment. Lily sat against a tree, facing the waterfall. Frank found a gigantic rock that fit him just right. They were both in their happy places and needed nothing else.

They both sat in their respective silence for an unknown amount of time. Lily sat listening to the soothing sounds of the water, she sensed loving beings around her. She knew she was in a sacred space and was welcome here. The beings closed in around her and placed their hands on her so that every inch of her body was covered. Quiet tones emanated from them, pulsing all around her, in a comforting and reassuring vibration. One came forward, who seemed to be the leader, and placed a hand on the top of her head. Words of blessing and acceptance filled her head. She then felt the warmth of healing light and love fill her. She accepted all that they were offering her. She quietly and humbly bowed to them in gratitude. They smiled and blended back into the natural surroundings.

Frank entered a deep meditation as soon as he closed his

eyes. He was at home here and comfortable with all around him, but this was the first time he'd brought someone else to his sacred space. It felt right to bring Lily here, as if he was guided to do that as well. He didn't have a particular intention to his meditation, as he often did. Today he only wished to ground, center, connect and receive whatever wisdom was available to him.

He connected with the beings that he always sensed here. The usual excitement and joy was heightened today. What was this about? He immediately knew the answer to his question was Lily. They were happy that he brought her to this sacred place. Joy and contentment filled him, and a slight smile crossed his face. He felt the presence of the beings around him, sending him light. One came in front of him and placed a hand on his heart and another on his head. An intense light shot through his heart, painful for a second then abating and revitalizing. His heart now radiated a love brighter and more expansive than ever before. He looked at this being hoping for an explanation. *You are healed. You are ready. All you search for is right here. Go forward without fear.* He felt the beings move away from him and recede back into the forest. He thanked them for everything he received, even if he didn't understand what it meant.

Frank and Lily opened their eyes at the same time and were caught in a mesmerizing gaze. Both shook their heads to break the contact and the spell that seemed to be over them.

"Hmm. I seem to have the most interesting experiences when I'm around you. I don't know why that is. I'm getting better at meditating and connecting, but this was so much more vivid and real, not only visually, but sensually and intuitively."

CHAPTER TWENTY-EIGHT

"What happened?"

"It seemed like this tribe of beings blessed me and welcomed me in. That's the best way for me to describe it."

He smiled. "I could feel their excitement. They were happy that you were here." He paused to consider his words. "You know I wasn't sure if I should bring you here or not. This is such a sacred place for me, and I wanted to honor that. But I felt like it was the right thing to do. Now it has been validated, I was right to bring you."

"I'm glad you did. This was such an amazing gift, not only with the beauty of this place, but to be honored and accepted by these beings. I don't have words." She blinked her eyes to keep back tears. "Thank you so much for sharing this with me."

Frank nodded, watching the waterfall and lush wilderness around it, not wanting to move quite yet. Something was shifting within him and he didn't want to rush the unfolding beauty or disrupt it. He sat for about 20 more minutes, when a dragonfly landed on his knee. It stayed for a minute or two, seeming to acknowledge him, and then flew away again. Message received.

"Are you getting hungry? Let's find a place to have our lunch." Frank looked around for a good spot to have a little picnic. They found a grassy spot where the sun was peeking through the trees to warm them. It felt good to be in the balmy sunlight. They both found their casual friendly banter return, and they laughed, talked and relaxed in the sunlight.

When it was time to go back, Frank suggested a different route. It would still get them to the car, but would show Lily another view. Lily was all for that. She had already taken tons of pictures, and was finding many more exciting shots to capture and document this magical day.

This trail wound around through the woods on a lower level than where they had come in. They were following the stream for most of the journey. "We'll have to cross the stream here." There were a series of rocks traversing the creek bed. The water looked to be about a foot deep, but was flowing fiercely. "Follow me."

Frank led the way from rock to rock. Lily followed, stepping exactly where Frank had stepped. He hopped across one section that was wider. She stopped, unsure if she could make it without falling in. "Take my hand, I'll help you across." Frank stretched his hand out for Lily to grab as she jumped. He caught her and pulled her onto the rock where he was standing. He pulled her right up against him to keep her from falling. Their eyes met, and their breath caught, electricity surging where they touched. Time froze for a moment. Several moments. Neither could look away. Captivated and breathless, they both broke the spell at the same time, coughing or looking away, and then moved to the next rock. The remainder of the hike was quiet and introspective.

"I have a couple of phone calls I need to make. Then we can decide what we want to do for dinner. We could cook something here, or go into town and sample the local fare."

"I think it would be fun to see what the town is like, if that is alright with you. I'd like to take a shower and maybe rest a bit while you are making your calls."

"That sounds great. Come down whenever you are ready."

Lily was grateful for a little time to herself. So much was happening, within her and around her, that it was hard to take it all in, much less understand it. Frank was such a dear friend. She treasured his friendship more than anything. She wanted to keep that relationship free and clear, and not let any illusions or fantasies cloud it up again. She set the intention that as she showered, the water would cleanse her of anything that was not true, clear or pure.

She emerged from the shower feeling clean, refreshed, reenergized, and at peace. She lay back on the bed to rest and fell asleep for an hour. The nap was much appreciated. She quickly dressed and set off to find Frank.

"Hey, I was just wondering if I needed to rescue you. It must have been a good shower."

"It was heavenly. It felt so good that I lay down on my bed and dozed off for a while. I'm sorry if I kept you waiting."

"No worries. You are on vacation here."

Frank's home was about a half hour from the city, but the nearest small town was only ten minutes away. The quaint little town held several small shops, a coffee shop, a bar, and two restaurants. "There is not much to pick from as far as restaurants go, but I really like this one. They serve delicious locally caught fish, and homemade breads and desserts."

"Perfect. I'm so hungry, I could eat just about anything."

They enjoyed the evening, going back to the comfortable and easy friendship. Lily didn't know what had transpired between them as they crossed that creek earlier, but she was glad that they had regained their relaxed rapport.

Discussing Frank's research and progress on his book,

she said, "I'd love to read that whenever you are ready to share, or if you ever want feedback. The topic fascinates me. I have always believed that at the core of all these cultures and religions, we are all the same and at the base it is love. Is that what you are finding?"

"There is that, but it's a little more complex when we are looking at their healing practices and beliefs as well. I haven't quite gotten to the basic beliefs behind all of that yet. It is taking me a lot longer than I expected. There is so much to look at and understand, and not all of it is written down. I'm hitting some roadblocks where I will need to meet with native healers because their practices are sacred and secret, they have never been told to others, sometimes not even in their own tribes, and definitely not to outsiders. There is nothing about them to be found in books. I may have to do some traveling to get the answers I am seeking."

"How exciting! That would be so much fun for you! How amazing to be able to meet with all of these ancient healers and learn from them!"

"Yes, it would be a dream come true. But figuring out how to make it happen is another thing. School will be starting soon, so I won't have the time I need to spend on all of this. I must also obtain permission and make all the arrangements to meet with these healers. And I need the funds to do all of this traveling. The scope of this project is much bigger than I originally thought, and I wonder what I have gotten myself into."

"How about doing a series of smaller articles about each practice? You could publish them one at a time, so that you continue to put something out in the media. Then you could set up some trips for when you have breaks, or maybe look at taking a sabbatical to travel and finish it up. If this is what you are meant to do, and it feels like this is something that is really important for you and lights you up, then you will find a way to do it. I believe things will line up as you need them, once you are clear and committed to it." Lily rested her hand on Frank's in support.

"You're right. I'm letting my frustration derail me. It will all come together, I just need to give it time. Initially, I had thought of just writing an article, but then decided to go all out and write a book. But you make a good point, I could start with the articles and then bring the information from the articles together for the book. Since my kids will be going to college next year, it may be easier to do the traveling then."

"I'll support you in any way that I can. Whenever you need me to give you a kick in the butt, I'll be happy to help!" Lily offered with a sly smile.

Frank chuckled. "You're too kind. I'll probably need to take you up on that a time or two though. I do appreciate your support."

Time passed too quickly, and when it was time for Lily to return home the next day, she was reluctant to go. "This has been the best couple days I've had in a long time. It was so much fun spending time with you, getting to know you better, and enjoying your beautiful home."

"It has been so wonderful to have you here. The time has gone so fast. I wish you could stay longer, but I know you have to get back to your life."

"I do have to work tomorrow. I would love to come back again sometime."

"Definitely. I'll give you my school schedule and maybe we can plan it around my next break, or almost any weekend."

"I can do that. I'll text you when I get back, and we'll talk soon."

They hugged goodbye, their bodies pressed tightly together as if merging into one. It felt different hugging Frank than anyone else. To hug him was to reconnect with a part of herself, a soul reunion of sorts. They hugged for a long time, neither one wanting to let go or sever the connection. Eventually, they did separate and Lily quickly got into her car. She drove away glancing at him in her rearview mirror, the longing in her heart and the sadness of leaving him causing a lump in her throat that she couldn't swallow. How could it be so difficult to say goodbye to a good friend after such a great visit?

Chapter 29

Soul, I had the most wonderful time visiting Frank. It seems like our friendship has reached a deeper level, there is such profound trust, respect and love. I've never had that with anyone else. Our connection continues to get stronger all the time. I feel like I am still clear about our friendship, and don't have any illusions or fantasies about it like I used to. It was really hard to leave him though. As I said goodbye, it felt like I was leaving part of myself behind. Is that what happened?

Look again, from the perspective of your heart and soul.

Ok, show me. (Closing her eyes, she saw the situation from a new perspective deep within herself.) Being with Frank I am connected with a part of myself that I have been missing most of my life. Being with him is like a reunion of our souls that I have been longing to get back. That's why it feels like coming home. I need to remember that we are still connected even when we are apart. Thank you!

~Lily's journal

Lily arrived home to her apartment a couple hours later. She immediately texted Frank to let him know she arrived safe and sound. She then texted Derrick to tell him the same. Her phone rang as soon as she sent the text.

"Hey beautiful, welcome back! How was your trip?"

"It was great! I had a wonderful time! The north shore is incredible! I'll definitely have to go back again and see more of it. I did a lot of hiking. I'm a little sore today and exhausted. I'm sure I'll be in bed early tonight."

"Will I still see you tomorrow night?"

"Yes, I'll see you for dinner. I'll come home from work and change and then I'll be over."

"I can't wait. I've missed you!"

"I've missed you too. I'll see you tomorrow." Lily hung up and realized that she actually hadn't thought of Derrick for a second while she was gone. She felt a little guilty about that. Now that she had talked to him, she did miss him. She hadn't seen him for a couple weeks now. It would be good to spend time with him again. What was this feeling in her gut that felt like she had swallowed a baseball?

Work was busy, causing Lily's muscles to ache, but the day passed quickly without giving her time to think about anything else. She rushed home to shower and change clothes before her date with Derrick. She wasn't sure if they were going out, or if he would be cooking for her, so she decided to dress up just in case.

With time to spare, a little time meditating would help her to clear away her busy thoughts, quiet her mind and settle her emotions. She sat, lit a candle, and closed her eyes. She imagined her work day floating away, then her thoughts followed. Emotions began coming to the surface ... fear, sadness, worry, doubt, pain, grief. What was this all about?

A few minutes later she felt calm and clear. She thought about Derrick, and that baseball reappeared in her gut. *Hmmm. What does this mean? Soul, is there something you are trying to tell me?* Feelings of dread and anxiety spread from her gut to her chest and throat. Something about seeing Derrick was kicking up her emotions. She still needed to go and see him. She was not pushing the emotions aside, but was acknowledging them for getting her attention. Curious as to what this was all about, she reconnected with peace and calm again, as she walked to her car.

Derrick greeted her at the door with a hug and a tender kiss. "God, it's good to see you! I've missed you so much!" He hugged her again. "You look terrific!"

"Thanks! I wasn't sure what the plan was for tonight, so I didn't know what to wear."

"I've got dinner almost ready. I made pasta, I hope that's all right."

"Perfect. I've actually been craving pasta lately. It's been a while since I've had it. Good choice."

"Would you like some wine? Tea? Water?"

"Actually, I think I will splurge and go for a little wine."

"Living on the edge tonight, huh?" Derrick teased as he winked at her.

"Just don't take advantage of me if I get tipsy after a couple sips," she teased back. She was hoping the wine would help her take the edge off. She was still a little anxious about being here.

They talked about work and their families, updating each other on what everyone was doing lately. Their conversation was light all through dinner, and she began to relax. They moved outside with their beverages. Lily had switched to water by this point, one glass of wine being enough for her.

"So, tell me about your trip."

"Well, this was my first time to the north shore, if you can believe it. I think I'm the only one to grow up in this state and not have visited there. I love the rocks on the shore, the sound of the waves. I told you we did a lot of hiking. Everywhere we went the sights were incredibly beautiful!"

"So where did you stay?"

"I stayed with my friend. He has a lovely house right on the shore. It's absolutely perfect! The waves lull you to sleep at night and the sun wakes you up in the morning. It's one of the most peaceful places I've ever known."

"Wait a minute. Did you say he? You went to see a guy? I thought you were seeing a girlfriend."

"I didn't think the gender of my friend was important. A friend is a friend. And we are just friends."

"So, you just spent two days with another man?" Derrick took a deep breath, trying to keep his temper in check.

"Yes. I swear nothing happened. We are just friends."

"Tell me about this guy."

"His name is Frank. He's 40 years old. He has two kids in high school. He works as a professor in a college up there. We met in the healing class I took a couple months ago and became friends. He knows about you and has no interest in me other than friendship."

"He may say that, but you would be naive to believe it. No man could be friends with a woman that he found attractive, without thinking about sleeping with her. Haven't you seen 'When Harry Met Sally'?"

"If that is true, then maybe he doesn't find me attractive, because this is strictly platonic." As the words came out of her mouth, she wondered if they were really true. There was nothing romantic going on, but there was more to their friendship than was usual.

"Either you are a fool to not see it, or you think I'm a fool to believe it."

Lily gasped. "I can't believe you would say that to me. Do you think I'm trying to cheat on you and pretend I'm not? I would hope you knew me better than that by now. I could not live with myself if I did something like that. I expected you to trust me. Trust me; I would not lie to you, and I would not do something like that." Tears filled her eyes, betraying the anger that was ready to explode.

Derrick slammed down his glass of wine. His ears were turning red as he struggled in vain to keep his emotions under control. "You've kept me at arm's length for too long. I'm tired of this game you're playing, keeping me waiting here for you to decide if you want to be with me, while you look for someone better." He looked straight into her eyes. "I would have done anything in the world for you, Lily. But my patience has run out. I'm done. I just can't do this anymore. One day you may realize what you had here and regret losing me, but I won't be waiting." He got up and left, going back into the house, slamming the door behind him.

Lily ran around the house to her car, not wanting to risk

going through the house. Tears were streaming down her face fast and furious now. She didn't even know if she could see to drive. She drove a couple blocks to a parking lot, where she stopped and let herself sob it out. Finally calm, she drove home, promising herself a hot bath when she got there, maybe even some of her favorite ice cream. What was it about ice cream that soothed a broken heart?

Chapter 30

Soul, even though I am not completely surprised about things with Derrick, it still breaks my heart to have it end like this. I really did love him, just not enough, apparently. It seems like since I couldn't make a decision about him, it was made for me. I guess it does make things easier for me in a way. I still grieve the loss of him, the loss of the relationship, and the loss of the dream he represented. This is the end of a chapter, isn't it? Now what?

Begin the next chapter.

But I'm not even sure what the next chapter is. How do I start?

One step at a time. You'll find your way. And you'll have help.

Thanks, I know you're right.

~Lily's journal

Working the next couple days helped Lily to keep her mind off her problems. But it wasn't helping her to heal, or to get any answers for herself. Some time away by herself was what the doctor ordered. She had a couple days off coming up, and if she could call in a couple favors, maybe she could extend it to four days. That would be almost like a real vacation!

She found a bed and breakfast near Bayfield, Wisconsin. It was on the south shore of Lake Superior. She thought it would be fun to compare it to what she saw at Frank's. She told Nicki and Maria where she was going, but otherwise no one else really needed to know. And she didn't really feel like talking to anyone else to explain her departure, or escape. She texted Frank to let him know she would be out of town, and that she wouldn't be able to talk for a few days. She wasn't ready to tell him about her split with Derrick yet. She needed a little more time to process it herself first.

The drive to the B&B was lovely. The breeze blowing through her windows as she drove helped to refresh her. She knew somehow this time away would be good for her. All summer she had been trying to connect with her soul and find out what her soul wanted for her. Little hints and nudges had been coming to her for months, but now it felt like she was on the edge of something bigger. Through her sadness and grief, she also felt excitement for what was coming.

The B&B was delightful. Decorated in the original style of the 150-year-old house, it held the old charm and character, but with added style and some modern touches. Lily loved it! Her room had an exquisite view of the lake and gardens outside the house. She could see a pond with a fountain and a bench under a tree. Flowers of every color were in full bloom in every patch of garden, sending the fragrant aroma wafting through the windows. A gentle breeze was coming off the lake, although noticeably calmer here, compared to Frank's side.

Frank. Thoughts of him had an immediate calming effect on her. She wondered what he was doing right now. She missed talking to him, but would hold off a few more days to contact him until she had more clarity for herself.

She took a long walk along the beach. The sandy beaches here were not the tumbled, round stone beaches of the north shore. There were some rocks, but more like one would expect to find at any lake. She walked awhile and then found a log on the edge of the water to sit on. Perfect place to reflect on her thoughts, or simply veg out.

She took some deep breaths, and felt connected to the sand beneath her feet, and the water around her, the cool breeze, and the trees rustling behind her. Calling in support and guidance from her soul, her angels, and all beings of light who were with her, she said, *"Please help me to see the bigger picture, beyond my pain and heartbreak, beyond my emotions. Help me to see my life clearly and without fear or judgment."*

She felt herself moving into a deeper consciousness, looking at herself from outside, a birds-eye view. Visions flashed through her mind of various times in her life, seemingly random.

Not random, look again.

The visions came again, but this time she noted a common thread. They were all times in her life when she was trying to be what others wanted her to be. She was trying so hard to meet their approval and be accepted. She was not happy, as much as she tried to be. It seemed like her efforts were never sufficient. She always felt like she wasn't quite good enough. How did this fit with what she was currently going through?

She saw herself shaping her life into what was expected of her, into what everyone thought she should do or be. Her life was a template created from what other people expected. And then she saw that template being used to match her with Derrick.

As she inhaled sharply, a realization hit her. *"I was with Derrick because it seemed to be what was expected of me. To marry a good looking, successful man, who has money, a nice house, a cabin, have a couple kids. Was that really ever my dream?"* She felt an uncomfortable knot form in her stomach. *"That vision felt superficial. It's not that those things would be bad, but they were empty. I need more than that. Not more in a material sense, but something more fulfilling. Something that reflects who I truly am."*

Gazing out over the water, seeing seagulls soar and light fluffy clouds float by, she asked herself, *"What is my dream? What does my soul really want?"* She closed her eyes and let her mind clear, waiting for fresh insight to appear. This time it wasn't a vision but feelings she received, a deep connection, a sense of belonging, of understanding, respect, love, partnership, fulfillment, passion, purpose. She saw an image of herself as a healer, helping others by using her gifts. She felt content, joyful, and complete. Was this her soul's dream? She felt a warm glow radiate from her heart, full and expansive … *Yes.*

She stood and walked along the shore, looking at rocks,

and the gentle waves that moved in and out steadily. A light bulb went off for her. *Maybe that was the answer all along, to focus on what makes me fulfilled, and consider everything else as just a bonus. When I am happy, fulfilled, and content with what I am doing, when I am living my own passions, and when I am following my soul's purpose, I won't need a man to do that for me. This is something I can do for myself!*

The rest of the day she did things that made her happy. She went paddle boarding, walked into town for lunch and checked out the shops along the way. Following her intuition and guidance, she browsed the stores, completely tuned in, happy, in the flow of goodness. She was looking through a bookstore when a new book jumped out at her, practically hopping off the shelf into her hands. It was about starting a purpose-driven business. This was what she needed, to learn what it would take for her to start a healing business. Trusting that everything she needed would be there when she needed it, it was becoming more apparent to her that she had been helped all along. She just hadn't been aware or paying attention to all the ways she was helped.

As she visualized her healing business, and what that would look like, she felt her confidence growing. Exhilaration swelled within her, and she felt herself beaming with joy. *So this is what it feels to be in alignment with your soul ... I could get used to this!*

With each day that passed, Lily felt more connected and in alignment with her soul and her purpose. She began writing down ideas and inspirations that came to her about her business. Her heartbreak was a faint memory, something that had to happen to get her to this new joy. She was grateful for this course correction in her life, and excited for what was to come.

She discovered a hiking trail that wound along the edge of a cliff, near the water, surrounded by trees. It would be amazing to sit there and meditate. But how did one get up there? There must be a path up the back side, likely a more gradual one. She ended up forging her own path, climbing treacherous rocks and steep terrain, to make her way to where she wanted to be. She hoped to find a better route on the way home.

She sat on the edge of the cliff, above the shore, leaning against a tree. It was the perfect spot and she claimed it as her sacred site. Letting her eyes close, she drifted off into meditation. In a vision, she was walking along a path. The path was smooth and easy, and bright light was shining at the horizon. As she walked, she was joined by another. They walked side by side, as equals, keeping each other company, supporting and encouraging one another. Looking down she noticed that they were holding hands as they walked together, happy, joyful, fulfilled and content.

Becoming aware of the waves below her, and the wind blowing on her face, she opened her eyes. *What did that mean? Do I need a partner? I thought that my soul purpose was something I needed to do myself.*

It is something that you do for yourself, but you don't have to do it alone. You can have support and encouragement from someone else, if you choose.

If I choose. So that means I don't need to think about finding a man right now. If the right one comes along, it wouldn't get in the way of my soul purpose to have his encouragement and support. He would need to be understanding of my purpose, that's important to me. Fulfilling my soul's purpose is still my top priority, followed by helping him to fulfill his.

An image of a shooting star streaking across the sky seemed to confirm her wish. The image remained, vivid in her mind. Only when she opened her eyes and saw that it was daylight with the sun high in the sky, did she realize it was just a vision. She sat on the cliff edge for a while longer to take in all the exquisite beauty. She also felt an uncontainable joy that all of her deepest dreams and desires were on their way to becoming a reality. It didn't scare her in the least, and for some reason, she just knew it was true, and right.

When she was ready to move on, she looked around for another way to get back, or at least a less difficult route. She walked along the edge of the cliff, where a couple of places looked like they could be foot paths leading down, or they could be caused by rain runoff. Which way should she go? She examined the path, and saw what looked like rocky edges for foot holds, appearing solid enough to support her. She felt confident that she could manage the challenge this presented.

She began her descent, taking time to make sure she had good hand holds. She was about halfway down when she reached a ledge. She stopped for a breather, and to drink a little water from her bottle. As she was standing there, catching her breath, the ledge she was standing on collapsed, and she was thrown into a landslide down to the shore. She was moving so fast that there was nothing she could grasp onto to catch herself. She heard herself scream as she went down.

A blood-curdling scream echoed across the shore. Zeke took off running in the direction of the scream. He found a woman lying on the shore, her legs in an unnatural position. He felt her neck for a pulse, and found her alive and breathing. He called to her but there was no response, she was unconscious. He dialed out for help on his cell phone. It looked like she fell from the cliff, feet first. Her legs were certainly broken. He didn't want to move her in case her spine was injured too. Since she was lying on sandy beach, he prayed that she would be ok, and that help would come soon.

Paramedics arrived in about 10 minutes. Zeke informed them of what happened and that he was a first responder. They stabilized her neck and carefully moved her onto a back board. She was still unconscious when they placed her into the ambulance. It was a difficult trek, but they made it up to the road without delay.

"Would you like to ride along? Hop in if you want to come."

Zeke jumped in without giving it a thought. He didn't know this woman, but somehow he just couldn't let her go alone. The paramedics were busy checking her vitals and making sure she was stable. Once those tasks were complete, they asked him questions about her. They were shocked when they learned he didn't know her and had just found her on the beach.

Frank suddenly felt weak in the knees, as a feeling of panic and pain flooded his senses, and he held on to the railing to keep from falling down the stairs. Lily. Something was wrong with Lily. The sense of disaster was so strong he couldn't ignore it. He tried to call her. No answer. He kept trying, but the phone kept going to voicemail. He texted her to ask if she was okay. He sent several more texts explaining that he had a sense that something was wrong, and to please call him so he would know she was safe.

Zeke heard her phone ring and then buzz repeatedly. He pointed this out to the paramedic. The paramedic said they couldn't answer it, but if he wanted to, they wouldn't stop him. Zeke saw the text asking if something was wrong. He could tell someone was worried about her, and since they didn't know who she was or who to contact, he decided to return call.

"Lily, thank god!"

"Sorry, this isn't Lily. My name is Zeke. Can I ask who you are and why you are calling her?"

My name is Frank Stillman, and Lily is a good friend of mine. I had a bad feeling that something had happened to her. I just had to call and find out if she was okay. Why didn't she answer?"

"She was in an accident near the shore. She fell and is unconscious, her legs may be broken. She's on her way to the hospital in Ashland now. Do you know anyone we should contact?"

"I don't. But I'll leave now and I should be there in about an hour and a half. Could you please call me if you have any news or if anything changes?"

Zeke thought for a minute before he answered. "Yes, I can do that."

"Are you one of the paramedics?"

"No, I just found her on the beach and called them."

"But you are still with her?"

"Yes, I just couldn't leave her alone and unconscious. I'll stay with her until you arrive. What is her name, so I can tell the doctors?"

"Her name is Lily St. Angelo. She lives in Minneapolis. She is a nurse, and I know she has good health insurance, no medical issues that I know of, is very healthy, and 33 years old. I'm grateful that you called me, and that someone is there with her. Thank you so much. Oh, by the way, what is your name?"

"Zeke. Zeke Garron."

"Zeke, thanks so much for staying with her. I'll be there as soon as I can." After Zeke relayed the information to the paramedics, he said another prayer: *"Please God, help Lily to be okay, to recover from these injuries. Don't let her die on my watch!"*

Chapter 31

I've come to believe that one can never truly know if
something is good or bad when it happens. What seems
like a tragedy can turn out to be the greatest blessing
later on. Often the most difficult moments in our lives
prepare us for the most amazing times yet to come.
Maybe it is true that you can't appreciate the light
without the dark. Thank you, soul and my angels, for
guiding me through them all!

~Lily's journal

Frank immediately got into his car and started driving. He used his cellphone to make calls while on the road. He called his ex to make sure the kids could stay with her for a couple days. He notified a colleague to let him know that he wouldn't be in. School hadn't started yet, but they were preparing for the semester ahead. He'd have to do that when he got back.

Once those details were tended to, worry set in. Thoughts began swirling in his head. What if ... what if ... He stopped himself. He connected with his soul, and to God and the angels. He asked for the healing light and love to come for Lily, to heal whatever needed repair right now. He envisioned her body being filled with bright light, and suspended in a healing state.

A knowing came to him. *She won't wake up until she is done with this phase of healing. It is benefitting her on all levels. She will be fine. When she recovers from this injury she will be stronger than ever. This was no accident, it happened for a reason.*

Frank arrived at the hospital in record time. He rushed in frantically looking for Zeke and Lily. A nurse guided him to where Zeke was waiting. "Zeke? I'm Frank. How's Lily?"

They were told one leg was badly broken and would need surgery. The other was broken at the ankle and put in a cast. She had no other injuries that they could find. Her head and neck were without serious injury, except for a concussion. She was still unconscious."

"Can I see her?"

"You'll have to ask the nurse."

"I can't thank you enough for all that you've done for us today. I really appreciate your help. Could I have your contact information, so that we can thank you properly when this is over, and we can also let you know how it all turns out?"

"I guess I can do that. I don't need any more thank you's, but it would be nice to be told when she recovers." He found a piece of paper and jotted down his number for Frank.

Frank wrote his cell phone number on his business card and handed it to Zeke. "And if there's anything I can do to help you, please give me a call. I mean that."

Zeke nodded and walked out the door. He came to the

ambulance, and realized his car was a half hour away. He could use a little help. Just then the paramedic he had spoken with earlier came by and saw Zeke standing by the curb. "Do you need a ride? We keep our rig parked in the garage in Bayfield and are on our way back there now."

Zeke gave a little nod to the heavens, smiled, and said, "Perfect timing. I was just wondering how I was going to get back there, and here you are!"

Frank found Lily in a room in the ER. "They will be moving her upstairs shortly," a nurse reported.

"When will she have surgery?"

"We don't know yet. Probably in the morning. Hopefully she will wake up soon, now that she has pain medication on board. We're thinking it is mostly shock that is keeping her out. Maybe she will wake up now that you are here."

Frank pulled up a chair next to the bed. He held her hand in his and sent all the love in his heart to her. "Lily, it's Frank. I'm here for you. Please wake up and talk to me. I miss talking to you. I miss everything about you since you visited me. Please wake up. There is so much I want to tell you." He leaned over and kissed her hand, and holding her hand to his face he continued to pray.

A couple hours later, Lily woke. "Frank?"

Frank had fallen asleep holding her hand. "I'm here, Lily. I was worried about you."

"How are you here?"

"That is an interesting story. But first, how do you feel?"

"My legs hurt really bad. Otherwise I feel ok. What happened?"

"What do you remember?"

"I was on the edge of a cliff overlooking the shore. I was trying to find a better way down. I found a small path leading down. It was steep but thought I could manage. There was a landslide. That's all I remember."

"A guy named Zeke heard you scream and found you on the beach. He called 911 and stayed with you until I got here. I was at home and had a sudden feeling that something bad had happened to you, so I called your phone several times, then texted your number, explaining why I was calling. Zeke found your phone and called me back. They didn't know who you were or who to call. I got in the car and came right away, and Zeke left after I got here. Is there anyone you would like me to call? Your parents? Derrick?"

"Not right now. You're the one I would have called, and you are already here. I'm really glad you came. I'll call my parents tomorrow after surgery, then they won't have to worry about me."

She was drifting off to sleep again; the pain medication was kicking in. "Frank, please stay with me."

"I'm not going anywhere. I'll be right here. Get some sleep." He kissed her hand and she was out. He was relieved she was okay and that she wanted him to stay. He couldn't imagine leaving her. This was where he belonged.

Frank slept in the chair next to Lily's bed, holding her hand, resting his head on the edge of her bed, careful not to disturb her. He heard her stir around 6am. When he looked up, she smiled at him. He felt the sun come out in that small smile.

"You're still here," she mumbled.

"Of course, I told you I would be. I am a man of my word." He smiled back at her. "How are you feeling?"

"Like I've been hit by a train. My legs really hurt."

"They should be coming in soon to get you ready for surgery."

"I'll be glad to get that over with. Right now, every little movement hurts, even when I breathe."

A nurse came in to prep her for surgery. They wheeled her in the hospital bed to the surgical unit. Once they arrived there, Frank was asked to stay in the waiting area. "I'll be waiting for you when you wake up." He squeezed her hand and kissed her on the forehead. Then she disappeared behind the automatic doors.

Lily asked that Frank be updated on her status when she was out of surgery, and that he be brought into her room as soon as possible. "I want his face to be the first thing I see when I open my eyes." As a nurse, she knew that unless she told them her wishes, they would not extend any such courtesies to Frank, since he was not family.

Everything went well, with no complications. She was moved into a private room. Frank was there holding her hand when she awoke. And as she wished, his face was the first sight to greet her. She smiled and squeezed his hand, before falling back to sleep.

A nurse was checking her vitals when she woke again. Frank was not there. "Where's Frank?"

The nurse reassured her, "He just went to the restroom. He's been holding your hand day and night since you arrived. You are very lucky to have someone so devoted to you. It's very sweet."

"Yes, I am lucky." Lily thought about Frank. She was so grateful that he was here. There was no one else she wanted with her. She felt comforted by his presence. She knew that as her good friend, he would be there for her. But to hold her hand day and night? Was that still friendship or was something shifting in their relationship?

Frank came back into the room. "Of course, I leave the room for one minute, and that's when you decide to wake up."

"It's okay, Frank. I knew you were still here, and I knew you were with me the whole time."

"Should we call anyone to tell them that you are in the hospital?"

"I should probably call my parents. They are in Arizona. And I should also call Maria, she knew I was coming here. And tell Nicki I won't be able to work for a while. I should leave a message for my supervisor, I'll need to be on medical leave for a while."

"Have you thought at all about what you want to do when you are discharged? You'll be laid up for a while, either in a wheelchair or crutches."

"No, I haven't thought about that. My apartment is upstairs, so that won't be possible for a while. I could go to a transitional care facility until I can return to my apartment."

Frank moved closer and clasped her hand, his eyes filled with love and compassion. "You could come and stay at my house for a while. The three of us could take care of you. Think about it. We would love to have you."

"But the guest room is upstairs."

"You could stay in my room, and I would sleep upstairs in the office. I could easily put a hospital bed in there if you need one, or you could sleep in the bed there. There is an accessible bathroom right off the master suite. Or if you prefer, I could carry you up to the guest room at night, and back down in the morning. Most days you would be on your own during the day. But I could be home whenever I don't have class or meetings. We would cook all the meals and do laundry. You could sit out on the patio and enjoy the sounds of the water and the fresh air to help in your recovery. It could work out well."

"That seems like a lot of work for you. And I would feel bad kicking you out of your own room. Why would you want to do all that?"

Frank held her hand in both of his and looked into her eyes. "I really enjoyed our time together when you visited. The house seemed so empty after you left. This is completely selfish, but I would love to have you there every day when I get home. And I think you would heal much faster and more comfortably with us than at a nursing home. You could relax listening to the waves outside, letting nature assist in your recovery. It will be perfect!"

Lily sensed there was more that he wasn't saying, but she wouldn't press him about it yet. His proposition was a good one, and he seemed to have thought of everything. It would be nice to spend a couple months recovering on the north shore, and to spend time with Frank would be a big plus.

"You're sure this is what you want to do? What about your kids? Won't it be weird if I just move in for a couple months?"

"They'll understand that the situation is a special circumstance. Besides, they liked you. They'll be happy to help you. It will be a good experience for all of us."

"Alright, you've convinced me. But promise me that if it gets to be too much for any of you, and you want your house back, that you'll let me know. We need to talk about this even if it is difficult. Our friendship is too important to have hurt feelings or resentment about something like this. I can easily go somewhere else, if or when I need to. Do we have a deal?"

"Yes, I can agree with that." Frank smiled, doing a little happy dance inside.

"And one other thing ... I want to help you with your research while I'm laid up. Whatever menial tasks you need done, I'll do them, since I need something to occupy my time. I'm really interested in your research, and you already said you could use a research assistant. I want to be able to repay you somehow for all that you are doing for me."

"You drive a hard bargain, but I guess I can live with that!" Frank smiled and kissed the top of her head.

"Now I just need to get out of here."

Frank stepped out of the room to get some lunch while Lily called her parents. They were concerned, but relieved that she was okay, and that she had a good plan for when she was released. They would be happy to have her stay with them, but she did not want to fly to Arizona. She appreciated the offer, but assured them she had it all under control.

Next, she called Maria. She explained what had happened and what her plan was. Maria was excited to hear that she was with Frank. "So, does this mean you are moving past the friend-zone?"

"Not yet. I'm not going to get my hopes up, but it does feel like things are shifting between us. He's been holding my hand day and night since he got here. No matter what it is, I just love being around him. If we stay friends like this forever, that would be just fine. I'm happy. Isn't it amazing how things line up? You would think that having an accident like this would be a tragedy, but I'm starting to think it is a gift."

"The universe works in mysterious ways. I'm glad you're ok. Thanks for contacting me. Let me know what you need from your apartment and I can get it for you and bring it up to Frank's."

"That would be a big help! And, hey, I know you are looking for a new apartment. Mine will be available for the next couple months. You're welcome to stay at my place. Then I won't worry about it while I'm gone."

"Really? That would be perfect. I was getting a little nervous about not finding anything yet. I'll pay you rent, just let me know how much."

"Consider your house-sitting services in lieu of rent. I've got it covered. Feel free to move in as soon as you like and make it comfortable for you. There's not a lot of storage space, but make yourself at home. I'm happy that you will be there. It is a relief for me to know my place is being taken care of. "

"Thanks so much, Lily! This is a huge help for me too. I'll be in touch."

She called her boss to notify her that she would be out for at least 8 weeks. Then she called her landlord to say she gave permission for Maria stay there and to ask him to give her a key. She also contacted the B&B to let them know what happened, and that they would be stopping by on the way home to get the belongings she left in the room.

All that talking and organizing was exhausting. She slept another two hours. A physical therapist came in to exercise her legs, get her up out of bed and into a wheelchair. She sat up for about an hour and then went back to bed. Another therapist came to assess her brain function, to see if she had any memory loss, or other problems as a result of the head injury. She passed with flying colors. Her doctor was amazed that she didn't have any cognitive issues after the concussion and being unconscious for so long. One more thing to be thankful for.

The next day she found moving around to be much easier, her pain was better controlled, and she had more energy. PT showed her exercises she could do on her own, and also taught her how to get out of bed without putting weight on either foot. She was managing the transfers from bed to wheelchair and wheelchair to chair or toilet with minimal assistance. She could go home with a wheelchair and would be set up with home therapy to continue her rehab. In a couple weeks she'd be able to bear weight on the left foot, and possibly switch to crutches.

While she was waiting for her discharge to be finalized, Derrick rushed in. "Lily, I came as soon as I heard. Oh my God, how are you? I've been so worried."

"How did you find out?"

"I went to the hospital to talk to you, but you weren't there. I asked one of your coworkers and she told me about your accident. I'm so sorry I didn't get here sooner."

"It was nice of you to come all this way. That was really sweet of you. You're lucky you got here when you did, because I'm about to be discharged."

"Great! Then I can drive you home."

"No. Derrick, I don't need your help. And may I remind you that we broke up."

"Lily, I know I over-reacted, and said things I didn't mean. I went to the hospital to try to get you back. I love you so much and can't live without you. Please forgive me."

"I'm sorry, Derrick. I can't go back. Even though you hurt me, I realized you did me a favor. I know that I have kept you at arm's length, and I couldn't understand why. I have been trying to figure that out all summer. I have done a lot of soul searching on this trip, and have a clearer understanding of what I truly want and need in my life. For too long I have been doing what everyone else expected of me. Since you left me, I am now free to follow my soul's passion and purpose. I feel better about myself than I have in years! Thank you for helping me to see that I need to live my life, and not let others live it for me. I'm sure you will find someone who can make you much happier than I ever could. I really do wish you happiness. I will always love you, but we are not meant to be together. Someday you will see that I am right."

"But Lily, I know we could be happy together, and have a really good life."

"Yes, you're right, we could. But I have realized that it wouldn't be enough for me. I need more than that. I need to follow my soul and my purpose, or I will never be fulfilled. I would never be truly happy without that."

"Is this about that other guy?"

"No, this is something I figured out on this trip by myself. I need to find my own happiness and fulfillment and not rely on any man to make me happy. I know that is hard for you to understand, but I am telling you the truth." She took a deep breath to calm herself. "I think you should go now. Thank you for coming."

"So that's it then. Nothing I can say to change your mind?"

"No, I'm certain. This is what I want, and what is right for me. I'm sorry, Derrick, I didn't mean to hurt you. I do wish you every happiness."

Derrick slumped, his pain and heartbreak apparent. "Goodbye Lily." With that, he turned and walked out the door. Lily felt bad for him, he looked so sad and dejected. But she knew in her heart that she was doing the right thing. As much as she cared for him, he was not the man for her.

Lily sighed in relief once he was out of sight. A weight had lifted from her to have explained all of that to him. She knew he was hurt, but now they could both move on.

Frank came back into the room. "Did you catch that?" She asked.

He nodded. "I'm sorry. I didn't mean to eavesdrop. I was about to come in and when I heard what was being said, I decided it was best to wait out in the hall."

"I'm glad you did. It wouldn't have been pretty if he found you here. He already thinks we were having an affair. That's what prompted our breakup. I'm sorry I didn't tell you earlier. I needed time to sort it out for myself. During the time I was up here, before my fall, I made some profound realizations about myself, my purpose and what I want to do with my life. I don't need a man to make me happy, I can do that for myself. I need to take responsibility for my own happiness and follow my soul and my purpose. Nobody else can do that for me."

"What do you want to do?"

Lily brightened as a hopeful smile crossed her lips, "I want to study healing, become more confident and proficient in that, and start a business as a healer."

"I can totally see you doing that and being very happy and successful. I'll do anything I can to support and encourage you in this. You really do have a gift that is needed in the world. It is important to honor that."

"Thanks. You don't know how much it means to me to have your support on this."

The nurse came in and finalized her release. They wheeled her down to Frank's car. She was happy to be out and moving on. They decided the backseat would probably be the best place for her to sit, where she could elevate her legs on the seat.

The trip home was long, with a couple stops. One stop was at the B&B to pick up her belongings. They borrowed a couple of pillows from the B&B to make her more comfortable. The pillows could be returned when they came back for her car. Another stop at a medical supply store was to rent a wheelchair.

Lily drifted off to sleep for a good portion of the ride. She woke when the car shut off in front of Frank's house. "We're here already? That wasn't so bad," Lily stated groggily.

"I'll go open the door to the house and then come back for you."

Lily wasn't sure how he was going to manage this by

himself, but she trusted Frank to figure it out. He wouldn't let her be hurt. He returned and opened the car door. She slid out feet first. Once she reached the edge of the seat, Frank put one arm under her knees and the other behind her back and picked her up.

"Oh my gosh. Are you sure I'm not too heavy?"

Frank laughed. "You underestimate me and my superhuman strength. I am more than just a pretty face, you know. Besides, you're a lightweight. I've got books that weigh more than you." He carried her into the house and gently set her on the couch with her legs stretched out. He immediately propped them up with pillows. "How is that? Are you comfortable?"

"Yes, this is perfect. Frank, I don't know how to thank you for everything you are doing for me. I really appreciate all your efforts. I hope it doesn't become a burden to you and your family since this is going to be probably 6-8 weeks." She reached for his hand, looking into his eyes to express her deep gratitude.

"Don't worry, I'm really happy that you are here. I mean that." He looked down at their hands.

"What is it? Is there something wrong?"

"Nothing's wrong, but there is something I need to talk to you about." He pulled an ottoman up next to her by the couch, so he could sit close without disturbing her position. "I feel like I need to tell you, but I am hesitant, because I don't want you to feel awkward now that you are here. I probably should have told you before we left the hospital, but I didn't want you to change your mind."

"What is it Frank? You're making me nervous."

"Things have been changing for me in the last few weeks. Since our last phone session, actually. That session really cracked me wide open. It was difficult and painful at first, but I have noticed myself being more aware of my feelings, and what I want. For the first time in years I am able to think about what would make me happy instead of just my kids."

"That's great! I'm so happy for you!"

"My heart had been closed off for so many years that I hadn't even been aware of it. It was like it had been in a coma, asleep for such a long time, and now that it is awake, it is starving for all it has missed out on." Still holding her hand, looking down, he paused to choose his words carefully. "Your visit here last week was the best time I've had in a long time. I don't ever remember enjoying being with anyone as much as you. And when you left, I felt so lost and alone. My kids even commented on my melancholy. They understood what was going on even before I did, or at least before I was willing to admit it. They were pushing me to do something about it too, but I knew you had Derrick and I didn't want to complicate things for you. Then when you got hurt, I was so worried and afraid of losing you. Afraid I had missed my chance." He looked directly into her eyes. She felt his pain and his fear, but also more.

He took a deep breath, gathering up his courage. "I realized that I am in love with you. Completely. Body, mind, heart and soul. I love you more than I ever believed possible. If you just want to stay friends, I can deal with that, but if ..." Lily grabbed his shirt and pulled him toward her, cutting him off mid-sentence as her lips pressed against his.

The moment their lips touched, they both felt a surge of

electricity flow through their bodies. Frank cupped her face in his hands and deepened the kiss. Behind their closed eyes they both sensed light radiating around them, similar to what they experienced in the session weeks ago when they were both in a space of love. Frank took a breath, his forehead resting against Lily's.

Lily was reminded of the dream she had about Frank a while back, of the two of them on the beach, with energy surging through them. She gasped as the lightbulb went off in her mind. "So that's what our souls have been trying to show us all along. I wonder if our souls could be laughing at how long it takes for us to get the messages. I thought it was just a dream or a fantasy."

"A dream come true, I'd say. Don't take this the wrong way, but I'm so glad you had that accident."

Lily laughed, "Actually, I am too. If I hadn't hurt my legs, I wouldn't be here right now. And there is no place in the world I would rather be. This is definitely worth a couple broken bones and a few days in the hospital!" They kissed again, tenderly, with love flowing freely between them. She had never felt anything so powerful. "You know, after two months of this, you may have a hard time getting rid of me."

"I'm already thinking there is no way I'm ever letting you go." He kissed her again lightly. "Maybe you could start your healing business here."

"Hmm ... we'll have to see. That idea definitely has potential, I'll add it to my possibility list." She pretended to ponder it coyly, but even as she did, she saw the vision she had before her fall. She was walking on a path surrounded by light, holding hands with an unknown man beside her. Now she could see his face, and it was definitely Frank walking beside her. Everything was becoming clear.

"I'm so glad we found each other and are now together on this path. This is what I've been searching for my whole life. Part of me always believed it was possible, but I never really expected to find it. I love you so much! I tried so hard not to, but now my heart is bursting!" Lily's eyes sparkled with light and joy as she spoke.

Frank pulled her tight against him, careful not to hurt her legs. "I feel the same way. I guess I just never knew what I needed. I had accepted my lonely life and told myself it was enough. I'm so happy to find I was wrong. Being with you just feels so right in every way. I've never been so completely happy!"

They continued to kiss, enjoying the expanded connection between them, and a depth of love and passion neither of them had ever imagined. Their souls smiled with joy and contentment, happy, connected, and at peace. They were exactly where they belonged. They were finally home ... their souls reunited, whole and blissfully happy ... though in many ways their journey had just begun!

About the Author

Kris Groth is a bestselling author with contributions in *"Courageous Hearts: Soul-nourishing Stories to Inspire You to Embrace Your Fears and Follow Your Dreams," "365 Days of Angel Prayers,"* and *"111 Morning Meditations."* Her inspiring articles also appear regularly in Aspire Magazine, Sibyl Magazine and The Edge Magazine. This book is her first novel and an expression of several of her passions; her love of reading & writing, love & romance, healing & transformation, angels & spirituality.

In her day job, Kris is an energy healer and spiritual mentor. She is passionate about helping people connect more deeply to their own truth, to promote healing and restore balance to the body, heart, mind and soul, and live a soul-connected life. Kris serves clients around the world through her healing and spiritual mentoring sessions, and powerful guided sound healing meditations using crystal singing bowls. Learn more at www.KrisGroth.com and claim your free *"Sacred Sound Healing Meditation & Affirmation 4-pt gift set."*

Other pursuits that bring Kris joy are: yoga, meditation, intuitive watercolor painting, going for walks in nature, skiing, dancing, reading, journaling, and spending time with her family. She lives in Minnesota with her wonderful husband, two amazing daughters, and a rescue dog named Misha, who is the princess in their little kingdom.

Kris would love to connect with you on social media:

http://www.facebook.com/bodywhisperstherapy

www.twitter.com/kris_groth

Sign up here to receive notices, special offers, and inspiring bits. I'll even throw in my ***"Connect to Your Soul Meditation"*** as a thank you gift.

For more information on all Kris has available to heal your heart, nurture your soul and illuminate your path ... healing and mentoring services, books, courses, meditations, etc. visit her website:

www.krisgroth.com

If you enjoyed this book, Kris would absolutely love for you to post a review! She heard another author say that wonderful reviews are better than dark chocolate, and no matter how much she loves chocolate, she believes it's true!

Acknowledgements

I am so grateful for all the unending love and support from my family... Mike, Kiara and Mackenzie. I couldn't have done this without you! Thanks for your encouragement, patience, and belief in me! I love you so much!

Thanks to my parents for instilling in me the belief that I can do whatever I set my mind to, and to always reach for my dreams.

I am so grateful for my publisher Shanda Trofe, whose teaching, guidance and support through this whole process made it do-able for me. A heart-felt thanks to Linda Joy for all her loving encouragement, assistance and support. This book would still be just a dream without the two of you, and I thank the divine for bringing us together. Thanks for helping my dream come true!

Thanks to all my teachers, mentors, coaches and friends, who have inspired me and cheered me on. I am also grateful for all those who have shaped my life and my work in immeasurable ways, both seen and unseen; hopefully you know who you are. My life has been touched by so many beautiful souls that I have been blessed to have come in contact with. I am so grateful!

I am eternally grateful for the divine guidance of my angels, masters and guides, "my divine writing team," who have inspired this book from beginning to end. I thank you for being present in my life each day, for gently pushing me in the direction of my soul, for the endless flow of abundance, and the boundless love that surrounds me.

And to all my readers ... love and gratitude from the depths of my soul!